MIRROR
MIRROR

MIRROR MIRROR

TWISTED TALES

by SILVERMAN

SCHOLASTIC INC.

New York Toronto London Auckland Sydney
Mexico City New Delhi Hong Kong Buenos Aires

First published in the United Kingdom in 2002 by The Chicken House,
2 Palmer Street, Frome, Somerset, BA11 1DS.

ISBN   0-439-44086-6

12 11 10 9 8 7 6 5 4 3 2 1   2 3 4 5 6 7/0

Printed in the U.S.A.   40

First Scholastic paperback printing, October 2002

Book design by Chad W. Beckerman

MIRROR MIRROR

CONTENTS

A child in the mirror sees a beast,
a beast in the mirror sees an outcast,
an outcast in the mirror sees a rebel.

A rebel in the mirror sees a coward,
a coward in the mirror sees a soldier,
a soldier in the mirror sees a captive.

A captive in the mirror sees a bride,
a bride in the mirror sees a gambler,
a gambler in the mirror sees a hero.

A hero in the mirror sees a child.

Yolande was older than her sister by two years. She dearly loved her sister, Camilla, and her sister loved her. They shared the same bedroom and in the solitude of night, when the rest of the household was drenched in sleep, they pledged to each other that their love would last forever and that whenever one of them was in need, the other would come to her assistance.

One Saturday afternoon they were on their way to meet friends. Strolling over the iron-railed bridge, they heard a boy calling to them.

"Hi, there!"

"Oh, no!" Camilla said. "It's Neil."

Neil wasn't one of their friends. There was something scary about Neil — the way he could be nasty to other kids, or hurt them, or the way he swore at teachers behind their backs. And his eyes always looked wild, as if he were hunting for ways to cause trouble.

DYING FOR FRANJIBELLE

"Hello, Neil," Yolande said. "We can't stop long. We're meeting friends in town at two o'clock."

"No problem," Neil said. "I just thought you might like to see something down there."

He pointed to the riverbank.

"What is it?" Yolande asked.

"Ever heard of franjibelle?"

"Never. What is it?"

"You won't believe your eyes," Neil said. "It's a flower that blooms only once every seven years. It has violet-and-red petals and it's huge." With his hands he formed a circle larger than the size of a dinner plate.

"Wow!" Yolande exclaimed. "Is it in bloom now?"

"Yes," Neil said.

"We can't come now!" Camilla urged. "We'll be late."

"Okay," Yolande said. "Perhaps another time, Neil."

"There's no other time!" Neil said. "Unless you mean in seven years."

"Come on, Camilla, let's go take a look," Yolande said. "It won't take long."

Yolande took Camilla's hand and they followed Neil down under the bridge and then alongside the broad, murky river. They walked for several minutes, until the old shipyard came into view, with its rusting cranes and abandoned warehouses.

"I thought it was just down here on the riverbank," Camilla said.

"It is," Neil answered. "Just a little farther."

They walked on until they reached a small cluster of trees. Then Neil turned off the path and crawled under a fence. He held up the barbed wire so that Yolande and Camilla could crawl through.

Under the trees it was much darker. As their eyes adjusted, Yolande and Camilla beheld a circle of young people sitting around on logs. They all seemed lost in their own thoughts and weren't speaking much.

"There it is," Neil said, pointing to a plant growing within the circle.

Yolande and Camilla approached the plant. The outermost rims of the huge petals were dark violet and their texture was velvety. Toward the center, where the petals joined, the violet merged to lilac and was flecked with red, as if someone had spilled drops of blood on it.

"Why don't you smell it?" Neil suggested to Yolande and Camilla.

Before they could respond, they heard a voice chanting:

"One sniff and you're in heaven.
Two and you're in hell.
Three, and leave the world forever
Dying for franjibelle."

The voice came from a sleepy-looking girl who was sitting on a log watching Yolande and Camilla.

"Let's go!" Camilla urged her sister.

"One sniff will be all right," Neil said. "Look. I'll do it."

He bent over the franjibelle and placed his nose near the center of the violet flower. Then he inhaled its powerful scent. Almost immediately, a smile spread over his face as if he were experiencing a delicious pleasure.

Without hesitation, Yolande did the same. Oh, how luscious that scent was! It rushed into her lungs — never had she felt anything more tingly and wonderful.

"Camilla, it's gorgeous," she sighed.

Camilla finally yielded. She, too, bent over the flower and inhaled its marvelous aroma.

"See?" Yolande said. "It's beautiful, isn't it?"

Neil led Yolande and Camilla to one of the logs and helped them sit down. He squatted beside them. Yolande threw back her head and laughed. She felt deliriously happy. She gazed up through the leaves and observed the sunlight streaming down. It fascinated her that she could actually see sunbeams. Millions of them. And each sunbeam was constructed from minute rectangles, each of which reflected rainbow colors. Yolande saw the sunbeams bouncing off leaves, the way rain bounces off a hard surface. She noticed how the leaves themselves were breathing. They were taking in great gulps of air, feeding the air through to the branches and trunks of the large trees. In so doing, they were making themselves green. Oh, it was

all so magical, with butterflies fluttering around weight-
lessly in the air. When she turned to her sister, Camilla,
how exquisite she looked! Like an angel, with her large,
black eyes. Even Neil, how sweet and innocent he was!
And what a lovely smile he gave her, as if to say, "Aren't
you glad I brought you down here?" Then she caught
sight of her own arms, with those soft hairs growing
in precise patterns. *What a strange creature I am,* she
thought. She took off her shoes and socks, admired her
ten peculiar toes, then stood up and began to twirl
around, moving from person to person, peering into their
eyes and laughing. The girl who had chanted the franjibelle verse joined Yolande in her dance. Yolande didn't
even know this stranger's name, but she already loved her
like a sister. They held hands and swung each other
around, laughing and shrieking with joy.

The girl, parting from Yolande, approached the franjibelle again and bent over for a sniff. Yolande followed
her. How mysterious the franjibelle now seemed! Like a
magic fountain springing from the earth to bring delight
to all who came under its spell. It was the source of all
happiness. Yolande bent over.

"No, Yolande!"

It was Camilla. She had run over to stop Yolande from
taking a second sniff. But she was too late! Already the
intoxicating aroma had filled Yolande's nose and lungs.

MIRROR MIRROR

"One sniff and you're in heaven.
Two and you're in hell.
Three, and leave the world forever
Dying for franjibelle."

The girl who had danced with Yolande was chanting
again, twirling herself around. This time Yolande didn't
join her. A profound nausea had taken hold of her and,
as if the weather had suddenly changed, she hugged herself to keep warm. Everything she saw now appeared
horrific. The trees were giant ogres with gnarled trunks
and vicious arms grabbing at the air. And why were there
so many horrible little bats flying around? Neil looked
unmistakably evil. *What was he up to?* Yolande wondered.
And her own sister, Camilla? Why was she so angry?
Yolande had never seen her look like that before! Her
eyes so cruel, her mouth snarling and deceptive. Was
Camilla a demon? Why had Yolande never noticed this
wickedness in her own sister?

These thoughts were interrupted by a pandemonium
of screams and yells. A gang of men, shouting and wield-
ing sticks, had invaded the secret hideout of the franjibelle sniffers. They rushed around the circle, catching
hold of some of the boys and girls sitting on logs and tying them up with ropes. A few managed to escape, running for their lives along the riverbank. For a moment,
Camilla had the chance to escape. There was a clear way

out if she ran for it. But Yolande was seized by a brutish man with an unshaven face who bound her hands and legs. When Camilla saw Yolande being captured, she hesitated. In that instant of delay, she, too, was overpowered by an enormous man wearing a black scarf wrapped around his head so that only his eyes showed. While Camilla was being bound, she noticed that Neil was neither captured nor making a run for it. Instead, one of the men was passing him a bundle of money, which he pocketed. "We'll come for more next week," the unshaven man said.

The captives, seven in all, were marched down a path in the opposite direction from the shipyard. They soon reached two vans that were parked on a gravel road. The captives were bundled into the vans, the men climbed into the front seats, and the two vans drove off at high speed. Yolande and Camilla were together in one van, bound fast, but instead of that bringing comfort to them, Camilla suddenly rolled over toward Yolande and bit her sister's arm. "It's all your fault!" she said. "We should never have gone with Neil, we should never have sniffed that evil flower. It's all your fault."

Yolande said nothing.

The van traveled for hours and hours. The captives were given neither food nor water. Night came and still the van sped on and on. By dawn, it became apparent that they were traveling through a mountainous region, because the van struggled on the steep hills.

Eventually, after a day and a half of nonstop driving, the van came to a halt. The back doors were flung open.

"Get out, all of you!" the unshaven man barked.

It was difficult for the captives to move with their arms and legs bound. They were weak from lack of food and water and from being cooped up in the back of the rattling van for so long. Despite that, the man roughly forced them to stand upright in a row.

Camilla looked around and saw that they were standing in front of an enormous mansion, set amidst lawns and ornamental gardens. The front door opened and a man, wearing dark glasses and a black leather jacket, strode out to meet them.

Solemnly, he greeted the unshaven man and inspected the row of captives. He stopped at Yolande, forced her mouth open, and examined her teeth.

"She'll do," the owner of the mansion said. "And these three."

The other three consisted of Camilla and two boys.

The man with the leather jacket handed over a wad of money to the unshaven man, who said, "Thank you, Mr. Axel." The three remaining captives were herded back into the van. It set off down the driveway toward the huge wrought iron gates that slid apart to allow the van to exit the property.

Yolande, Camilla, and the two boys were left alone with Mr. Axel.

"You all work for me now," he bellowed. "From now on you will obey my every command! Is that understood?"

Mr. Axel pulled out a long, curved knife from his belt. Yolande was petrified! What if she were murdered here in this unknown place?

Mr. Axel approached the captives. But instead of doing them injury, he cut the ropes that bound their hands and feet.

"There is no way out," he explained. "The perimeter walls, as you can see, are extremely high. The gates are controlled by my security guards. They have orders to never let any of you out into the world again. So you better get used to it here. I expect loyalty and hard work from each of you. In return, you will be housed and fed."

The captives were shown to their quarters, one dingy room for the two sisters, and another for the boys. Though there were no beds, just a skimpy mattress on the stone floor, Yolande and Camilla were so tired they fell asleep immediately.

Their lives at the Axel mansion were miserable. A daily grind of cooking, serving, fetching, and cleaning, with never so much as a single word of kindness from Mr. Axel. On the contrary, they were often punished for the most trivial mistakes, confined alone in a dark room in the basement without food for three days.

How many years they spent slaving at Mr. Axel's mansion they never knew, and all the time they were there, they were never a comfort to each other. That was the most intense pain of all. Every minute of every day, Camilla burned with rage and bitterness. She blamed Yolande for what had befallen them, and, in time, the sisters grew to hate each other as much as they had once loved each other.

Every month, Mr. Axel hosted an extravagant party. These parties were a terrible ordeal for the servants. Gargantuan feasts had to be prepared for the guests, who arrived wearing bird and animal costumes, and who ate and drank and danced right through the night, before driving off at dawn in their sleek cars. Whole pigs were roasted on spits, long tables were laden with every sort of exotic food imaginable, and countless bottles of liquor were consumed. The servants worked all night until their feet and hands were blistered. But they were never permitted to sleep until the mess that was left after the banquet had been cleared away.

During one particularly riotous party, Mr. Axel provided his guests with a treat that Yolande and Camilla immediately recognized. He placed a large flower with velvety violet petals in the center of a round table. It was a franjibelle!

The guests approached the flowers and, after the first sniff, were soon mesmerized by its effects. They laughed ecstatically, skipping and dancing around the ornamental gardens. After the second sniff, fierce arguments and scuffles broke out between the costumed guests. They threatened one another, swearing and cursing violently. After the third sniff, they began to feel faint, vomiting, stumbling, and falling to the ground, unconscious.

When dawn broke, Mr. Axel and all his guests lay like corpses wherever they had fallen. It was eerie and silent, like a battlefield after a dreadful slaughter.

Yolande, seeing an opportunity to get some shut-eye before the cleanup, sneaked off to her room. But she hadn't been asleep long when her sister, Camilla, came barging in.

"Now's our chance," she said.

"What?" Yolande asked irritably, for she was very tired. She thought Camilla was spiteful to wake her.

"We must get out of here!"

"I'm too tired to go anywhere," Yolande groaned. "I've been working all night. I'm exhausted. Let me sleep."

"Yolande!" Camilla called out. "Yolande! Don't close your eyes! Wake up!"

She shook Yolande roughly, trying to stir her sister.

"Yolande!" Camilla shouted, lifting her sister into a sitting position. "Let's get out of here."

Yolande rubbed her tired eyes. Eventually, she opened them and looked around. Who were all these boys and girls slumbering dreamily around her? She recognized one of them. It was Neil. They were all sprawled out on logs under a cluster of trees.

"You shouldn't have sniffed the franjibelle twice!" Camilla said. "Come on! We have to go! Our friends are waiting for us, remember! We have to meet them at two o'clock!"

"What is it now?"

"Quarter to," Camilla said. "Come on. If we hurry we can just make it."

Camilla helped Yolande put on her shoes. Then she helped Yolande to stand.

"You're not going already, are you?" Neil said, rousing himself for a moment. "How about another sniff of fran-jibelle?"

"No, thank you!" Camilla said. "We have to go now."

Camilla supported Yolande as they left the circle of people and staggered through the trees back to the river-bank.

Behind them they could hear a chanting voice:

"One sniff and you're in heaven.
Two and you're in hell.
Three, and leave the world forever
Dying for franjibelle."

14

Cynthia lived in a faraway city and thought she had a perfect life. Both her mother and father loved her very much. They lived happily, all three together. Her mother helped her to make a patchwork quilt, and her father built her a tree house. Sometimes they took her on a picnic or went to the movies with her. It was all great fun, and she loved her mother and father as much as they loved her.

But there came a time when Cynthia's father and mother began to argue and fight. Night after night, they called each other all the names under the sun.

"You big oaf!" Cynthia's mother called her father. "You can't just have your own way all the time!"

"Who are you to complain?" Cynthia's father replied. "You're never nice to me anymore, you stupid cow!"

"How dare you call me that," Cynthia's mother shouted. "You stupid clod!"

"You should talk, you old bag!" Cynthia's father retorted.

And so it went on, night after night, week after week, month after month, and year after year. These squabbles always ended with Cynthia's mother crying and Cynthia's father marching out of the house, slamming the front door, and not coming back for hours. It made Cynthia miserable to realize that her mother and father no longer loved each other. She hated hearing their arguments.

In the end, Cynthia's father and mother decided to separate.

"But only on one condition," Cynthia's mother said.

"And what's that?" Cynthia's father asked.

"That Cynthia lives with me."

Cynthia's father's face turned red as it swelled with rage.

"No! She lives with me."

"But I can give her more love!" Cynthia's mother insisted. "A girl needs her mother."

"That's not true, you selfish woman!" Cynthia's father yelled. "I can give her just as much love, and a girl needs her father."

"You liar!" Cynthia's mother fumed. "I love her more and she stays with me. You wouldn't even know how to look after her."

And with that, she grabbed hold of Cynthia's left arm and pulled Cynthia toward her. Immediately, Cynthia's father grabbed hold of her right arm and pulled as hard as he could.

"I love her more!" shouted her father.

"I love her more!" shouted her mother, even louder.

Cynthia's father and mother pulled and pulled, but neither was able to pull Cynthia out of the other's grasp.

Cynthia, as you can imagine, wasn't enjoying all this. It was starting to hurt a lot!

"You're only doing this to get at me!" Cynthia's mother bawled, and she pulled twice as hard as she'd been pulling before.

"You only want to punish me!" Cynthia's father responded, and he pulled twice as hard as he'd been pulling before.

At that moment, Cynthia's grandpa came in from the backyard garden.

"He's stealing my Cynthia!" her mother yelled.

At first, Grandpa was confused. But when he understood what was going on, he hobbled over to help Cynthia's mother.

"That's not fair!" Cynthia's father exclaimed.

The front door opened and in walked Uncle Sid, who was coming to visit.

"Help me, Sid!" Cynthia's father bellowed. "She belongs with me."

Sid rushed in and took the side of Cynthia's father.

"I love her more!" Cynthia's mother shouted. "Let go!"

"I love her more!" Cynthia's father yelled. "You let go!"

If only they would have noticed how much all this

was hurting Cynthia, they might have stopped. Tears of pain were streaming from Cynthia's eyes.

But no! They all pulled and yanked and tugged and heaved. And they made such an awful noise, the neighbors heard and came running in.

Mr. Sprig, their neighbor on the left, joined Cynthia's mother's side, and Mrs. Dewar, their neighbor on the right, joined Cynthia's father's side.

"She's staying with me, you vile ape!" Cynthia's mother screamed. "You only care about your job."

"No way, you freak!" Cynthia's father answered. "You care only about your appearance. She's coming with me!"

Cynthia could barely stand the pain. She felt as if her arms might pop out of their sockets if they pulled any harder.

Cynthia's mother used her cell phone to call her sister.

"Come over right away!" she pleaded. "It's an emergency. I need you."

Soon Cynthia's aunt Jude and her boyfriend, Wesley, arrived. They began to pull on Cynthia's mother's side.

With two extra people, it seemed certain that they would win, but Cynthia's father used his cell phone to call his friends Luke and Andy.

When they arrived, they joined Cynthia's father's side, and the contest evened out again.

"Let go, you animal!" Cynthia's mother whined.

"No, you let go, you evil eyed witch!" Cynthia's father wailed.

Nobody even noticed that Cynthia was weeping and weeping, her agony almost unbearable.

Cynthia's mother looked around to see if she could get extra help from anywhere.

"Come and help us, Beatrix!" she called to her bull-dog.

The bulldog waddled over and tugged at her belt. The extra weight was helpful to Cynthia's mother's side.

"Here, Butch! Help my side!" Cynthia's father called to his rottweiler.

The dog ran over and added his weight to Cynthia's father's side.

Poor Cynthia sobbed and sobbed. The pain was overwhelming.

The noise of all this pulling and tugging and yanking and heaving and shouting and screaming and yelling and bellowing was finally heard by a policeman passing the house outside.

"Hey!" he said. "What's going on in here?"

"He wants to take my daughter away from me!" Cynthia's mother screamed.

"She's lying!" Cynthia's father roared. "She wants to take my daughter from me!"

"Well, I tell you what," the policeman suggested. "Let's

be fair about this. I'll draw a line here on the floor and when I say, 'Ready, set, go!' both sides will pull. Whichever team pulls the other over this line is the winner, and the daughter will stay with that person. Is that clear?"

Cynthia's mother and father both agreed. Nobody heard Cynthia's desperate protest — she was so frightened.

"Okay now — Ready, set, go!"

Both teams pulled and yanked and tugged and heaved.

At first, Cynthia's mother's side appeared to be winning and almost pulled Cynthia's father's side over the line. But then Cynthia's father's side had a fresh burst of energy, and they almost pulled Cynthia's mother's side over the line.

Nobody noticed that Cynthia was in a terrible state.

The contest continued evenly for a while, with both sides pulling and yanking and tugging and heaving, until suddenly, both sides pulled so hard that they split poor Cynthia right down the middle!

There was a terrible shriek of pain, then each team fell noisily into a heap on different sides of the line.

Cynthia's mother was still holding the left half of Cynthia, and Cynthia's father still held Cynthia's right half.

Cynthia's heart, however, fell out of her body and landed exactly on the line.

The policeman picked it up and placed it in a plastic

bag. "I'll place this heart in safekeeping, thank you very much," he announced. "And I now declare that the left half of the daughter belongs to the mother and the right half to the father. This proves again how fair the law is."

Cynthia's father was happy with the outcome. He stormed out of the house holding Cynthia's right half.

"At last!" he said. "We can go find somewhere else to live."

"I don't want to go anywhere without my other half!" Cynthia's right half shouted.

But her father ignored her and kept on going.

Cynthia's left half remained with her mother.

"We can be quite happy on our own," her mother said.

"But I want my other half back!" Cynthia's left half cried.

"Hush! Hush!" her mother said. "Let's give it a try."

Cynthia's father bought a condo in the center of the city where he and Cynthia's right half could live. He bought her lots of presents and paid for her to have singing lessons. But it was so difficult to buy clothes for half a daughter or to have a sensible conversation with half a daughter.

Cynthia's mother tried to bake cakes with Cynthia's left half, and she encouraged Cynthia to plant a vegetable garden. But Cynthia's mother also found it difficult to have a good time with half a daughter or to find a suitable school for half a daughter.

Neither of Cynthia's halves was happy. Neither could get used to being just half a person. And without a heart, neither Cynthia's left half nor her right half was able to enjoy anything anymore.

At her mother's house, Cynthia's left half had to hop, hop, hop to her school or to the store or to the park, and she found it difficult to make friends. Cynthia's left half was so unhappy, she cried many tears from her left eye.

At her father's condo, Cynthia's right half had to hop, hop, hop to a different school or to a different shop or a different park, and she also found it difficult to make friends. Cynthia's right half was as unhappy as her left, and she cried many tears from her right eye.

Oh, how her left half and her right half missed each other! The left half wrote long letters to the right half, explaining how much she missed her. And the right half replied, writing long letters in which she spoke about the good times they used to have when she was one person.

Perhaps they would have lived separately until both of Cynthia's halves were old ladies, wrinkled and using a walking stick to hop wherever they wanted to go. But one day, Cynthia's mother was sitting downstairs in the kitchen when she noticed drip, drip, drip — the ceiling was leaking! She rushed upstairs to find Cynthia's left half weeping so much that there was a deep puddle of tears on the floor!

"This has to stop!" she said, comforting Cynthia's left half. "I will contact your father immediately."

She did. But the phone at Cynthia's father's condo just rang and rang.

Cynthia's father was busy wiping up a puddle of tears that Cynthia's right half had just wept. Eventually, he answered the phone.

"Listen to me," Cynthia's mother said. "This situation can't continue. We must glue Cynthia's two halves together again."

"Well, you bring your half here," Cynthia's father suggested. "Then we'll fit them together again."

"No way!" Cynthia's mother objected. "You bring your half here."

"Never, you nitwit!" Cynthia's father said.

"You're the same stubborn fool you always were!" Cynthia's mother replied.

There was an awful silence.

Then Cynthia's left half said to her mother, "What about my heart?"

And Cynthia's right half said to her father, "Why don't we all meet at the police station?"

So that's what they did.

"We've come for our daughter's heart," Cynthia's mother explained to the policeman at the front desk.

"You'll both have to sign for it," the policeman said.

Cynthia's parents signed the heart register. The policeman went downstairs to the vault, which he unlocked with a large key. There in the vault was a glass case and in the glass case was Cynthia's heart — still beating!

"Here it is!" the policeman said, handing it over. "Still in good shape."

"I'll take it," Cynthia's father said.

"No way, you dog!" Cynthia's mother shouted. "Give it to me!"

"Never, you sow!" Cynthia's father yelled.

"Excuse me," the policeman butted in. "I will handle this matter fair and square."

He made Cynthia's mother stand on one side with Cynthia's left half, and Cynthia's father stand on the other with Cynthia's right half.

"Now, wait for my command."

The policeman searched in his first-aid kit for a tube of special glue that policemen always keep handy for these occasions.

"Okay," he said to Cynthia's mother and father. "Now carefully bring your daughter's two halves together."

As they did so, the policeman slipped Cynthia's heart in. It fit snugly. Then he glued her two halves together.

Cynthia's parents were pleased to have their daughter whole again. They thanked the policeman for his help.

"It's all part of my job. I'm glad to have been of service."

Cynthia and her parents turned to leave.

"From now on," Cynthia's mother said to her father, "she will live with me and you can have her every second weekend."

"No way, you pig!" Cynthia's father protested, grabbing Cynthia by the right arm. "She's coming to live with me and you can have her every second weekend."

"You rat!" Cynthia's mother snarled, taking hold of her daughter's left arm.

As they began to pull, Cynthia's two halves began to come apart again.

"Ouch!" Cynthia cried. She called for the policeman, who came running with the tube of the special glue. He ordered Cynthia's parents to stop tugging. When they had loosened their grips, he glued her two halves together where they were coming unstuck.

"Can I keep that glue?" Cynthia asked. "It may come in handy."

"Certainly," the policeman answered, giving her the tube.

Cynthia walked out of the police station with her mother and father. Immediately, Cynthia's mother wanted to turn left, whereas her father wanted to turn right.

"She's coming home with me first!" Cynthia's mother screamed.

"She's not!" Cynthia's father bellowed. "She's coming with me, you shrew!"

"Listen!" Cynthia said. "If you both don't stop screaming, I'll seal your mouths shut with this special glue. From now on, you are going to stop calling each other names or I won't live with either of you."

Cynthia's mother and father were startled. They looked at each other and wondered how on Earth they could change their ways.

"All right," her mother said. "Let's flip a coin to see who she goes with first. Heads it's you, tails me."

"That's fine!" her father agreed. "I'll flip a coin."

From then on, Cynthia spent some time each week with her mother and some time each week with her father. She was able to be a whole person no matter who she was with. Never again was she torn in two. And her parents didn't dare scream at each other, at least, not when Cynthia was around!

In the years that followed, her wounds began to heal. But even to this day, she still has a scar all the way down her middle, reminding her of where she'd once been split in half. However, her heart has grown stronger with every hour that's passed, and she now believes she has a good chance of living happily ever after.

Craig and his brother, Mike, lived with their mother, who had a night job. Each evening when she went off to work, she hugged them and always said the same thing:

"Don't open the door and don't go out,
There's plenty of danger and trouble about."

Then she would give them each a kiss and say:

"Look after yourselves, no need to roam,
Stay happy and snug until I come home."

These words always kept the brothers warm and cozy until their mother returned sometime after midnight. Craig was the older of the two brothers, so he was supposed to look after Mike. And mostly he did. They would eat their dinner, watch some TV, then Mike would go up to bed. Craig would stay up for a while, fooling around with this and that, and then he, too, would go to sleep. Later, they would hear the familiar sound of the key in the front door. Their mother would come upstairs, peep in each of their rooms, and say:

> *"I'm home at last, are my boys all right?*
> *I love you both, sleep well, good night."*

But one dark and dreary night, their mother was in a rush to go to work.

"Oh, dear! Oh, dear!" she said. "I must hurry! Where's my coat?"

She found her coat with the fur collar, pulled it on, and ran out of the house without hugging or kissing her boys or speaking the words that kept them warm and cozy until she returned.

A short time later, the doorbell rang. It was Doug, an older boy from up the hill who carried a knife in his pocket. One day, he had shown Craig and Mike how he could spin it up in the air and catch it again by the handle.

"Come on out," Doug said. "We'll have fun."

"No," Craig replied. "I have to look after my brother."

"Bring him along!" Doug said.

"I don't want to go out," Mike said.

"Come on!" Craig said. "It'll be fun."

So Craig and Mike put on their jackets and out they went into the dark and dreary night.

Their first stop was a liquor store where they met up with Lloyd, who pretended to be old enough to buy alcohol. Craig and Mike waited outside.

A while later, Doug emerged carrying a couple of beers.

"Here!" he said, passing one to Craig.

Craig lifted the bottle to his lips and swallowed some of the bitter-tasting drink.

"Give some to the kid!" Doug said.

"No way!" Craig replied. "He's too young."

So Craig drank the rest of the beer. He felt woozy by the end of it.

Doug and Lloyd drank without seeming to feel anything. When they had finished the first beer, they drank another. And another. The more they drank the noisier they became, swearing and bragging and boasting.

"Let's go rob a house!" Lloyd suggested.

Doug agreed, so they all walked to a house up the road. Craig was a bit wobbly and he could barely walk a straight line. He felt sick. Lloyd and Doug weren't much better. From time to time, they staggered against walls or tripped on the sidewalk.

"Number seventy-three," Lloyd said. "The owners are away."

"You two keep watch," Doug said to Craig and Mike. "If anyone comes, whistle!"

Lloyd and Doug went around the back of the house. Craig and Mike heard glass breaking.

"Let's go home!" Mike urged. "I'm cold!"

"We can't go now," Craig said. "When they've robbed the house we'll go home."

"Okay," Mike said. "I'm tired."

After what seemed like a long time, Lloyd and Doug came out of the front door of the house. Lloyd was carrying a video camera he had found in the house. Doug was carrying keys. He used them to open the garage on the side of the house. Then he opened the door of the car that was parked inside, started the engine, and backed out.

"Climb in!" Doug said.

"We have to go home now," Craig said. "My brother's cold and tired."

"No problem," Doug said. "I'll drop you off at your house."

"But you're drunk!" Craig pointed out. "You shouldn't drive."

"Who says?" Doug said. "I'm fine. Climb in!"

"I don't want to," Mike whispered to Craig.

"It's just a short ride to our house," Craig replied.

So Craig and Mike climbed into the back of the car. Lloyd sat in the front next to Doug.

Doug revved the engine until it roared. Then he drove off at high speed. But he didn't go anywhere near the neighborhood where Craig and Mike lived. Instead, he drove them through the city, screeching around the curves. It was a wild ride, and Mike was frightened.

"I told you, I'm a good driver!" Doug boasted.

Doug drove the car past the dock area, then up through the mall's parking lot.

Craig noticed a car behind them. He realized they were being followed.

"Police!" he shouted. "Stop, Doug, or we'll be in a lot of trouble!"

"Nah!" Doug said. "We'll lose them."

He swung the car suddenly to the right, went the wrong way around a rotary, and then turned off down a street of stores. He thought he'd lost the police, but when he looked around, there were the flashing lights still following them.

By the time he turned his eyes back on the road again, the car had swerved onto the sidewalk with a huge jolt. Doug tried to swing the car around to avoid crashing into the stores, but somehow the car swung around too much and rolled over. It rolled and rolled, then crashed into a brick wall.

Glass shattered, a few bricks came tumbling down, and smoke rose from the car in the yellow streetlights. Then there was silence.

Craig was hurt. There were lights flashing on and off. Craig drifted up out of the car. He was floating. He floated above the car. He could see it there in the yellow light. He could see Doug and Lloyd running off. And there was Mike, lying motionless on the backseat. And still Craig floated. If he moved his left hand, he floated to the left. And if he moved his right hand, he floated to the right. If he lifted his head, he flew upward, and if he looked down, he flew downward. And now he was so high, he could see the city below him, with its tall office blocks, rows of houses stretching away in the distance, and then the countryside in darkness.

But what was that flying toward him? As it approached, Craig could see it was a man in a black cloak, heading in the direction of the crashed car.

"Hey! Where are you going?" Craig asked.

"To get the kid," the cloaked figure answered.

"But you can't!" Craig shouted.

"Give me three good reasons why I can't!" the figure said.

Craig was confused. He couldn't think of anything.

"You're too slow. See you later!" the figure said, and flew down toward the car.

Craig hovered where he was for a while. Then he moved his left hand and flew over the docks, across the mall, toward the house they had lived in with their mother and Jeff, their dad. That was before Jeff walked out on them.

He floated down, down, down to the house and drifted in through the back window, his old bedroom window, where he could see a young boy sitting on the bed. It was himself when he was younger.

Jeff, his dad, came in and said to the young Craig, "Hi, there! How are you doing?" The young boy hugged his dad and said, "Dad, please don't walk out on us. I'll always love you."

"Who said I'm gonna walk out? I'll never do that," his dad said.

"Oh, yes, you will," the boy said. "You're gonna go to Canada and leave us here."

Jeff said good night to the young Craig and went out of the room.

Craig floated out of the bedroom to the porch and watched his father go into the big bedroom where his mother was. Then he heard them arguing. "Don't touch me!" his mother screamed. Eventually, Jeff said, "I've had enough of this. I'm going to Canada."

As his dad came out of the big bedroom, Craig floated toward him and said angrily, "See! I knew you were going to leave!" Jeff put his arm around the young Craig and said, "Good luck, son!" Then Jeff took a small model of a starship out of his pocket and gave it to Craig. "Take care of Mike for me, won't you? I love you both."

Craig heard his mother sobbing and weeping. The front door shut as Jeff walked out forever and ever and never came back.

Craig put the model starship in his pocket, then

floated up out of his bedroom window. He could see his dad driving off, heading for the airport. He flew across the city until he saw below him a woman walking on the sidewalk in the dark and dreary night, wearing a coat with a fur collar. She reached a house, put a key in the door, and stepped indoors.

That's our mother! Craig thought. *And that's the house where we live now.* He lowered his head and flew down, down, down to the house and in through his bedroom window.

His mother came up the stairs, peeped in his bedroom door as she always did, and Craig heard her say:

> *"I'm home at last, are my boys all right?*
> *I love you both, sleep well, good night."*

But when she looked in Mike's bedroom, she gasped in shock.

"Mike? Where are you?" she cried.

She came running back into Craig's bedroom.

"Where's Mike?" she asked. "Is he all right?"

"I know where he is," Craig mumbled, tears rolling down his cheeks.

"My darling child!" his mother wailed. "Why didn't you take care of him?"

"I'll go get him back!" Craig mumbled.

"Here," his mother said. "You may need this."

She gave him a harmonica, the one Mike liked to play. Mike played the harmonica well.

Craig put the harmonica in his pocket with the model starship his dad had given him. Then he raised his head and floated up, out of the window, into the night sky.

"Bring Mike back safely to me!" he could hear his mother crying.

Craig floated over the city. He flew across the mall, high above the yellow streetlights, until he saw someone. It was a boy, running along, looking behind him as if the devil were chasing him.

Craig lowered his head, and down, down, down he flew until he was hovering over the boy. It was Doug. When he saw Craig floating in the air above him, he tripped and went sprawling onto the sidewalk.

"It's all your fault!" Craig said.

"It wasn't!" Doug replied. "I'm a good driver! It was the car's fault! Something was wrong with the steering!"

Craig floated closer toward Doug.

"Don't you dare touch me!" Doug said, pulling the knife out from his pocket.

Craig wasn't frightened. He suddenly flew toward Doug and kicked the knife out of his hand. Then he floated down and picked up the knife himself. He put it in his pocket, next to the model starship his dad had given him, and the harmonica, given to him by his mother.

Craig floated up into the night sky. He could see two

policemen running after Doug and catching him. Craig floated across the docks. Eventually, he saw the crashed car way below him. Would he be in time? He lowered his head and floated down, down, down, through the open rear door, into the crashed car.

Oh, no! The man in the black cloak was lifting Mike from the seat.

"Leave him alone!" Craig said.

"It's too late!" the man said. "I already have him in my arms."

Craig was desperate. He tried to pull Mike out of the man's grip, but it was impossible.

"Please don't take my brother away!" Craig shouted.

"Give me three good reasons why I shouldn't!" the man said.

"Because his dad loves him, his mother loves him, and I love him!" Craig screamed.

The man in the cloak hesitated.

"Why should I believe you?" the man asked.

"Please!" Craig pleaded. "These three things prove it." Craig took the model starship, the harmonica, and Doug's knife out of his pocket and showed them to the man.

"All right, kid," he said. "But next time I won't be so soft."

He placed Mike on the backseat of the car. Then the cloaked man climbed out of the car and flew off into the night sky.

Craig was relieved. He rested his head on Mike's shoulder.

A while later, he slowly became aware of sirens whining. Red lights were flashing.

"This one's coming around now," a voice was saying. He was being lifted onto a stretcher.

"Where's Mike?" Craig asked. "Is he all right?"

"I'm here," Mike said. He was in the ambulance, bandaged. "Can we go home now?"

"Okay, you two?" one of the ambulance men said, climbing in and shutting the doors. "We're going to the hospital now to have you checked over. We phoned your mother. She'll meet us there."

In a city to the west of everywhere lived a man with two sons, Luke and Vincent, and a daughter, Fran, the youngest, who was her father's delight.

The man had been stricken with a terrible illness. Doctors examined him and prescribed various treatments, each without success. They declared there was nothing more they could do to save him. He had just a few more months to live.

"Surely there must be a cure for this," Fran said to her brothers. "A remedy somewhere that would help."

"I doubt it," Luke said. "The doctors have tried everything."

"If the doctors can't save him," Vincent said, "nothing will."

When their father became so ill that he could barely sit up in bed, Fran finally persuaded Luke to go search for a remedy.

Luke didn't want to leave the city. He enjoyed hanging

out in bars and nightclubs. He didn't like being sent on a wild-goose chase, but he figured that he'd be back soon enough. His father provided the young man with a lot of cash and advised him to spend it wisely.

Luke boarded a train headed east. He traveled overnight to a small town at the edge of the wilderness. His backpack filled with supplies, he set off toward an area renowned for its medicine men. After several days, he found himself in a desert, where the only plants that grew were round cactuses, flat cactuses, hairy cactuses, and prickly cactuses. Day after day, he trudged along but saw no other person. He had soon consumed all the food from his backpack and was forced to hunt small desert creatures and drink cactus juice. But he never managed to fill his stomach, and what he longed for more than anything was a good meal. Finally, he reached a lumpy outcrop of mountains known as the Devil's Backbone.

"At last!" he said. "A little shade and maybe a rabbit for lunch."

About halfway up the mountain, he stumbled over a smooth rock. Or at least he thought it was a rock, until, on closer inspection, it turned out to be an egg.

How extraordinary the egg was!

Larger than an ostrich egg, with a shell as transparent as plastic wrap. Inside the egg was a pinkish jelly in which a strange creature lay curled. Its eyes were closed, but clearly its heart was beating and blood circulated through its arteries.

"What a piece of luck," Luke said. "Here I am, without a decent meal for weeks and what did I find, but just the kind of egg that would make a wonderful omelette. But how can I cook it without a decent frying pan?"

From his backpack, he took out a telescope that he raised to one eye. He surveyed the surrounding countryside. A long way off he saw a small building in a valley.

Hastily, he made his way down the Devil's Backbone into the valley. Above the front door of the building was a sign: LAST CHANCE SUPPLY STORE. He stepped inside.

"What can I do for you?" the storekeeper inquired.

"Do you sell frying pans?" Luke inquired.

"Sure do," the storekeeper said.

He waded through the shelves of sleeping bags, thermal underwear, and pocket knives to the wall on the opposite end of the store where canoes were hanging alongside flashlights and kettles. He pushed these aside and there, sure enough, was a frying pan. *But how small it is,* Luke thought.

"Don't you have something larger?"

The storekeeper searched again, and on another wall he found a frying pan twice the size of the first.

"That's better," Luke said, "but a larger one would be better yet."

"Well, we may have something bigger around in the back," the storekeeper said.

Luke heard the man clattering around in the store-room. Finally, he emerged with the largest frying pan that Luke had ever seen.

"This big enough?" the man asked.

"Yes, that will do nicely," Luke replied. "How much does it cost?"

The price was very high.

"But that's all the money I've got," Luke said.

"Listen, mister, you won't get another frying pan like this until you've crossed the desert. It's solid iron."

"Okay, I'll take it."

Luke gave the storekeeper all his money and strapped the frying pan to his back.

The return to the egg was extremely strenuous, not only because it was uphill, but because of the enormous weight of the frying pan. He was within sight of where he had left the egg when he heard the sound of hooves. Twelve men were approaching on twelve black horses. They were masked bandits!

"What have we here?" they asked one another.

"Looks like enough for an evening meal."

Luke quaked in his boots.

"You can't eat me!" he wailed.

"Why not?" one of the bandits replied. "Food isn't easy to come by in these here parts."

"Pleaoo," Luke said. "I'm not very tasty."

"There's only one way to find out," one of them said, and the others chuckled.

"What's that on your back?" a bandit asked.

"A frying pan," Luke answered. "If you let me go you can have it."

The bandits laughed. "The evening meal comes complete with its own frying pan! Fried meat tonight, lads!"

"Please . . ." Luke begged.

"Well, we could let you go if you hand over your loot!"

"I don't have any left," Luke wailed.

"Tough luck, sonny boy!" one of them said. And they carried him, pan and all, to their den on the northern slope of the Devil's Backbone.

Back home, Luke's father was becoming anxious. With every day that passed he grew feebler.

"Luke's been away a long time and still no word from him," he said.

Vincent, like his older brother, didn't want to leave the city. He enjoyed accompanying his older brother to bars and nightclubs. But without his brother it wasn't much fun. So off he went. His father gave him the same amount of money he had given Luke and the same advice to spend it wisely.

Vincent boarded the train that took him east to the small wilderness town. Then he followed Luke's trail until he found himself in the same desert where the only plants that grew were round cactuses, flat cactuses, hairy cactuses, and prickly cactuses. Finally, he reached the Devil's Backbone where he, too, stumbled over the large egg. He noticed the creature curled inside it, with its closed eyes and beating heart.

"What a piece of luck," Vincent said. "Here I am, starving, and what did I find but just the sort of egg that would taste wonderful hard-boiled. But how can I cook it without a decent pot?"

From his backpack, he took out a telescope that he raised to one eye. In the valley, he saw the Last Chance Supply Store. Down the mountainside he ran, imagining to himself how delicious the large egg would taste.

"Do you sell pots?" Vincent inquired.

"Sure do," the storekeeper said, and, after much searching, he produced a small pot.

"Don't you have something larger?" Vincent inquired.

The storekeeper found a pot twice the size of the first.

"That's better," Vincent said. "But a larger one would be better yet."

From the storeroom, the storekeeper brought out the largest pot that Vincent had ever seen.

"This big enough?" the man asked.

"Yes, that will do," Vincent said.

When he heard how much it cost, he hesitated.

"Listen, mister, you won't get another iron pot like this around here."

"Okay, I'll take it."

Vincent gave the storekeeper all his money and strapped the pot to his back.

Weighed down by the enormous pot, he staggered up the mountainside. He had almost reached the egg when he heard the sound of hooves. Twelve masked bandits were approaching on twelve black horses!

"Look, lads!" one of the bandits shouted. "Tonight's evening stew comes complete with its own pot!"

"Please don't eat me!" Vincent begged.

"Do you have any loot to buy your freedom?"

"No," Vincent wailed. "I spent it all on this pot."

"Tough luck!" The bandits laughed. And they carried him, pot and all, to their den.

With no news of either Luke or Vincent, their father grew increasingly anxious about the fate of his sons. He was now so ill, he had difficulty breathing.

"Should I try to find them?" Fran asked her father.

"No, not yet," her father said. "A girl out on the roads! It's too dangerous."

But Fran insisted. She didn't want to leave her father. But she was anxious to go and find a remedy that would restore him to good health.

In the end, he relented. Ill as he was, he provided her with the same amount of money each of her brothers had received and advised her to spend it wisely.

Fran took the train east, then crossed the wilderness,

following the trail of her brothers. After several days, she came to the desert, where the only plants that grew were round cactuses, flat cactuses, hairy cactuses, and prickly cactuses. Finally, she reached the Devil's Backbone where she, too, stumbled over the large egg.

How extraordinary! Fran thought as she examined it closely. She was fascinated by the small curled-up creature she could see in the center of the egg, with its closed eyes and beating heart.

"What a piece of luck," she said. "I must wait here until it hatches, for surely something marvelous will come from this."

From her backpack, she pulled out her sleeping bag, which she wrapped around the egg. Then she lay huddled down against the egg and waited patiently.

How long she slept, she would never know. But she was woken by the sound of clattering hooves. There before her were the twelve masked bandits on their twelve black horses!

"A girl this time!" one of the bandit's exclaimed. "Today's our lucky day, guys!"

"We've eaten two men," he explained to Fran. "And now it's your turn, unless you have money to buy your freedom."

"I do," Fran said.

"How much?" the bandit inquired.

"Enough," Fran said, and she handed over her wallet.

The bandits greedily divided the notes among themselves.

"Not bad," they said. "We'll spare your life. But you still have to come with us to our den to be our maid."

"Never!" Fran said.

They were just about to take her by force, when one of them noticed the large lump in her sleeping bag.

"What's that? Take it out!" one of the bandits ordered.

"No!" Fran said.

"Open it up or you're done for!" a bandit yelled, and they all pulled out their guns and aimed at her.

Carefully, Fran lifted the egg out of the sleeping bag. The bandits could barely hide their excitement.

"What an egg!" they shouted. "Let's take it back to our den and fry half in the pan and boil the other half in the pot."

"You will not!" Fran said. "Because it's just about to hatch."

Sure enough, just then, right in front of their eyes, the transparent shell began to crack!

A claw poked through. Bits of shell broke away. Jelly seeped from the egg onto the ground. A second claw poked through, followed by a tail! Then the egg snapped in two and the rest of the creature rolled out onto the ground.

It was scaly and pink and black. The creature began to uncurl itself, rising onto its legs, then standing upright. Slowly, it unfolded its body until it was as tall as a man! Finally, the lizard creature straightened up its head. And what a head it was! With huge, gleaming, round eyes, darting to the left and right, and a forked tongue that shot out of its mouth every now and then.

Fran and the bandits could barely believe their eyes!

But if they were surprised by its appearance, they were flabbergasted when it began to speak to Fran.

"I am Ixpetz, the Bright-eyed. You saved my life; now I will help you. Let us walk."

The twelve masked bandits thought about blocking its way, but Ixpetz shot out its forked tongue and emitted an earsplitting hiss.

The bandits placed their guns back in their holsters.

Ixpetz, the Bright-eyed, spoke again to Fran:

> *"Keep me always within your sight,*
> *Let your footsteps follow my track.*
> *Turn neither to the left nor to the right*
> *And never look back."*

Then Ixpetz walked boldly past the masked bandits. Fran followed close behind, keeping her eyes fixed on the creature. The bandits stood, rooted to the spot, and didn't try to stop them.

Once they were safe, Fran told Ixpetz about her father who was languishing with a terrible illness.

"The doctors can't help him," she explained. "I must find a remedy, otherwise he'll die within a few months."

She then told Ixpetz about her brothers, how they had failed to return home and were now missing.

"Come!" Ixpetz said. "First, we will find your brothers. Then we will see about healing your father."

Fran was filled with hope. She knew there was a remedy somewhere that could cure her father, and if anyone could help her to find it, it was this extraordinary lizard.

After some time, they came to an abandoned mine shaft cut into the mountainside. Ixpetz entered the darkness. Fran followed. The smell was awful, a mixture of horse manure and unwashed socks and underwear. There were twelve filthy sleeping bags in a row, and Fran realized that this was the bandits' den.

Beyond the sleeping quarters stood a huge pot and a huge pan. Next to each of these was a pile of bones. Ixpetz, the Bright-eyed, stepped up to each pile and blew on it. Instantly, Fran saw her two brothers, Luke and Vincent, standing as whole as ever. She was amazed to see them alive again.

"Whew!" they said. "That was a close call. We were nearly eaten by bandits."

When the brothers laid eyes on the giant lizard, however, they almost fainted.

"What's that?" they whispered to Fran.

"That is Ixpetz, who has saved our lives," Fran replied. "Now it's going to help us find a cure for our father."

"Let us walk!" Ixpetz said.

"We'll just take some of the bandits' loot before we go," the two brothers said.

They seized handfuls of money from the tin box in which the bandits stored their stolen wealth. Ixpetz shot out its forked tongue and emitted an earsplitting hiss. The two older brothers hurriedly pocketed what they had grabbed and left the mine shaft.

They walked for what seemed like weeks. The brothers, weighed down by the coins, grumbled about the difficulties of the journey. Eventually, they all emerged from a canyon to the open plains, where they found themselves in the middle of a war. Two armies were spread out as far as the eye could see, one in red uniforms to the left and the other in green uniforms to the right. Tanks, missile launchers, cannons, and guns were firing from left to right and right to left.

Ixpetz, the Bright-eyed, strode directly between the two armies.

"Where are you going?" Luke yelled.

"You can't just walk out in the middle of a battlefield!" Vincent shouted.

But Ixpetz shot out its forked tongue and emitted an earsplitting hiss.

"Keep me always within your sight,
Let your footsteps follow my track.
Turn neither to the left nor to the right
And never look back."

So Fran, Luke, and Vincent followed as closely as they could.

When they were about halfway across the battlefield, it occurred to Luke that the red army's cause was just. He veered off to the left and joined in the battle. At precisely the same time, it occurred to Vincent that the green army's cause was just. He veered off to the right and also took up arms.

"Your brothers are hasty to meet their fate," Ixpetz said.

Luke and Vincent fought for the opposing armies all day, and by evening both had been severely injured.

In the meantime, Ixpetz walked on and Fran followed.

The next day, an ambulance carrying the wounded overtook them. Ixpetz hailed the driver and asked to see the injured men. Luke and Vincent were in there but showing no signs of life.

Ixpetz, the Bright-eyed, blew first in Luke's ear, then in Vincent's ear, and both brothers leaped out of the ambulance.

"Whew! That was a close shave," they said. "We were nearly killed in battle."

Fran was grateful to see her brothers once again restored to life.

Ixpetz led Fran and her brothers beyond the commotion of the battlefield. Soon, they were alone again in the midst of a desert, where the only plants that grew were round cactuses, flat cactuses, hairy cactuses, and prickly cactuses. For what seemed like an age, they wandered here and there, the brothers becoming more and more irritable in the merciless heat of the sun.

"I'm thirsty," Luke said. "I'm tired of cactus juice."

"And I'm sunburned," Vincent said. "Will we never find shade?"

"We must keep going!" Fran insisted. "Ixpetz promised to find a remedy for our father."

The brothers moaned to each other as the days passed. And as they became hungrier and thirstier, their moods worsened.

"Ixpetz doesn't know where it's taking us," Luke said.

"It's as lost as we are," Vincent added.

Perhaps Ixpetz, the Bright-eyed, heard their grumbling, but all he said was:

> *"Keep me always within your sight,*
> *Let your footsteps follow my track.*
> *Turn neither to the left nor to the right*
> *And never look back."*

Not long after this, an astonishing sight greeted Luke's eyes — an oasis up ahead to the left, with elegant palm trees surrounding a clear pool of water. A beautiful woman, wearing a swimsuit and sunglasses, lounged on a beach chair. In her belly button was a glittering topaz.

"Brother, my luck has changed!" Luke said.

"Mine, too!" said Vincent, for at that moment he, too, spied an oasis, up ahead on the right, where another girl lounged on a beach chair. In her belly button a sapphire gleamed.

They ran off, Luke to the left and Vincent to the right.

Ixpetz shot out its forked tongue and emitted an ear-splitting hiss.

"We will return for you in three days," Ixpetz shouted.

Fran followed Ixpetz across the sand.

"Your brothers stubbornly refuse to learn," Ixpetz said. "But you have done well. I will now teach you the five secrets of lizard magic."

During the next three days, on a high dune, Ixpetz, the Bright-eyed, showed Fran how to walk on the earth without leaving a trail, how to see without looking, how to avoid danger by remaining motionless, how to be awake while sleeping, and how to seek advice from the lizard-spirits.

Fran learned eagerly and Ixpetz was pleased.

"Let us go rescue your brothers one last time," it said.

"And tomorrow I will give you the remedy for your father's illness."

Ixpetz led Fran through the deserts until two garish buildings came in sight. The building on the left was called "Luke's Casino" and the one on the right, "Vincent's Casino." In the lush gardens of each was a turquoise swimming pool surrounded by elegant palm trees.

But what a wailing could be heard coming from within each casino!

Ixpetz and Fran entered Luke's Casino first. Inside, the woman with a topaz in her belly button was wailing beside a coffin.

"He's dead!" she cried.

Fran looked in the coffin and saw Luke.

"What happened?" she asked the woman.

"He was shot by gamblers," she replied.

Ixpetz, the Bright-eyed, leaned into the coffin, blew in Luke's ear, and immediately Luke jumped out of his coffin, alive and well.

"Whew!" he said. "That was a close call."

Then they all went across to Vincent's Casino, where a similar scene was taking place.

"Vincent is dead!" the woman with the sapphire in her belly button wailed.

"What happened?" Fran asked.

"He was shot by moneylenders."

Ixpetz blew in Vincent's ear and immediately Vincent jumped out of his coffin.

"Whew!" he said. "What a narrow escape!"

Fran was glad to see her brothers alive again.

"Let us walk!" Ixpetz, the Bright-eyed, said. "We are nearly at our journey's end."

He headed out across the sand. Fran followed.

"We can't leave here," Luke whispered.

"We'll return after we've delivered the remedy to our father," Vincent agreed.

Ixpetz shot out its forked tongue and emitted an ear-splitting hiss.

"Keep me always within your sight,
Let your footsteps follow my track.
Turn neither to the left nor to the right
And never look back."

The brothers followed Ixpetz. But how difficult it was!

"Oh, no!" Luke said. "Not the desert again!"

"At least back there we had a life of luxury," Vincent added.

The two brothers still followed Ixpetz, but their pace slowed considerably.

"This isn't a good idea," Luke said. "We could make a fortune in those casinos."

"I agree," Vincent said. "Every minute wasted is money lost."

Their walking came to a stop. They could no longer contain themselves. They turned around and looked back!

But what did they see?

No oases! No casinos! No palm trees! No swimming pools! Nothing!

Only a barren desert with round cactuses, flat cactuses, hairy cactuses, and prickly cactuses.

"What happened?" Luke asked.

"Where has it all gone?" Vincent howled.

They ran back across the barren desert, searching the endless sands.

"Where's my casino?" Luke called out. "I'm sure it was just about here."

"I think mine was in front of that sand dune," Vincent replied. "Or was it on the other side?"

Fran could hear their voices growing fainter as they disappeared into the distance, searching this way and that for their lost casinos. But she never once looked back.

Ixpetz walked onward and Fran followed. The next evening, they reached a sunken valley, scattered with stone ruins.

Ixpetz crossed the stone maze until it reached a garden, where the strangest cactuses that Fran had ever seen were growing. Ixpetz cut leaves and branches from sevcral of these before proceeding to the stone circle at the center of the maze. Ixpetz asked Fran to light a big fire.

"This is a place of dancing," Ixpetz, the Bright-eyed, said. Ixpetz laid the leaves and branches on a flat stone that was being heated by the flames. Then Ixpetz began to move around the circle, stomping its feet.

A giant lizard dancing is an amazing sight! Ixpetz waved its tail and lifted its head to the dark sky and sang, "Ahuya! Huya! Huya!" Ixpetz spun around and sang, "Aheeya! Heeya! Heeya!"

Fran felt her own legs aching to dance! She wanted to join in! So she did. She danced, twirled, and stomped, and joyfully she sang, "Ahuya! Huya! Huya!" She spun around and sang, "Aheeya! Heeya! Heeya!"

The dancing continued for much of the evening, but suddenly Ixpetz stopped, taking Fran by surprise. Ixpetz placed the dried-out cactus pieces in a stone bowl and ground them into a powder with a stone pestle.

"Here is the remedy for your father," Ixpetz said.

"Thank you! Thank you!" Fran said, with tears of gratitude welling in her eyes.

"I have brought you to this place," Ixpetz said. "The rest is up to you. The time has come for me to journey on alone."

The words pained Fran. She was stunned. She had grown fond of Ixpetz and did not wish to be parted from the creature. But Ixpetz shot out its forked tongue and emitted an earsplitting hiss.

"No!" Ixpetz said. "You must find your own way from now on!"

And with that, Ixpetz stepped into the heart of the fire. The flames flared up all around — as high as the stars and moon — orange and green and mauve! The whole desert was lit up by the blaze.

Fran stood and stared. Sparks cascaded out in all directions. It was amazing! Fran gazed at the searing flames that leaped into the night sky, and, as she did so, their brightness entered her own eyes. The longer she stared, the brighter her eyes shone, until they gleamed as brilliantly as the fire itself. Even when the flames eventually died down, Fran's eyes were still glowing.

It was only then that she realized how tired she was. She lay down on the stone ruins and slept. She was alone. There was not a single trace left of Ixpetz, the Bright-eyed.

The following morning, Fran gathered the healing powder into a leather pouch and left the ruins, walking west, determined to return to her father with the remedy before it was too late. She had no one to watch out for her now. But knowing the five secrets of lizard magic, she felt confident.

During the day, the desert was scorching hot; at night, it was freezing cold. She knew there were bandits out there, snakes and spiders with deadly bites, as well as ravenous coyotes and vultures. One desert hill looked much like another — it was easy to get lost or travel in circles without knowing it. But Fran walked without leaving a trail, she saw without looking, she avoided danger by remaining motionless, she kept awake at night while sleeping, and she sought advice from the lizard-spirits.

In this way, she survived. Several days later, she reached the town at the edge of the wilderness. She boarded the overnight train and finally arrived back in the city to the west of everywhere.

People stopped to stare at her — they had never seen anyone with such large, glowing eyes! They moved aside as she approached. Fran, the Bright-eyed, had returned!

She made her way quickly through the familiar streets toward the hospital, where she found her father on the brink of death. His face was ashen, his eyes were closed. She took some powder from the pouch. She smeared it on her father's forehead and on the palms of his hands.

After a while, he opened his eyes.

"You have returned, dear child," he said.

"Yes, father, and I have returned with a remedy that will make you well."

He embraced his daughter and wept tears of joy.

The city where Hedley lived, like most other cities, sprawled out in all directions, had a huge number of inhabitants, and had streets that were always busy. For Hedley, it was home. He lived there with his father, mother, and younger sister, Serena.

Their comfortable house overlooked a subway station and from his upstairs bedroom window, Hedley could see the rush of commuters setting out every day for work. Each evening he would see them all return. It was like the tide of an ocean going out and coming in every day, waves of people flowing first in one direction, then the other.

One day, Hedley noticed a boy no older than himself sitting on the sidewalk outside the station. There was a scruffy dog beside the boy and a cap laid upside down in front of him with a few coins sprinkled in it. The boy looked like he didn't wash very often, and his clothes were shabby.

The boy was there again the following day and every day after that. Sometimes he sat there with his dog next to him, or he talked to the newspaperman, an old man with no teeth, who sat at a little table most of the time, selling the daily papers.

Hedley never spoke to the street boy, but he saw him every day on his way to and from school. Hedley also watched him from his upstairs bedroom window.

Very few people threw coins into the boy's cap, but some did, and every now and then the boy would remove most of the coins and slip them in his pocket. At night, the street boy slept in the doorway of a store that was boarded up and empty. He lay on a few sheets of cardboard and slept in a dark green sleeping bag that had seen better years.

Hedley's parents had also noticed the street boy.

"This area's going downhill," Hedley's father complained.

"They shouldn't be allowed to beg here!" his mother grumbled.

But the boy was always there, and near him, his faithful dog. The dog never wandered off on its own. It was a white terrier with black markings. Actually, the dog was not that white. More like yellowish brown. Once, Hedley saw them share a bag of chips.

When Hedley's parents asked him what he wanted

for his birthday, which was only a few weeks away, Hedley answered, "A dog."

"A dog's out of the question," his mother said. "No one could look after it when we're at work and you're at school."

"Why don't you ask for a bike," his father suggested. "Then you could ride to school."

So Hedley said, "Okay, a bike."

"I want a bike, too." His little sister, Serena, pouted.

But before his birthday came along, the weather turned freezing cold. There was a shimmering of frost on the grass in the morning, and puddles turned into sheets of ice that cracked if you stepped on them. Flurries of snow fell from time to time. Hedley wore his fur-lined parka and put on gloves and a scarf to go to school.

The street boy huddled in his sleeping bag during the day, hugging his dog closely for extra warmth. Hedley thought it was unfair that the boy should be out there in the freezing cold.

"Can't we help him?" he asked his parents.

"I don't think so," his father said. "It's his choice to live out there on the streets."

"Can't we at least give him some warmer clothes?" Hedley persisted.

"No!" his mother said adamantly. "Then he'd never stop pestering us for more."

The severe cold continued for sixteen days. A biting north wind added to the misery of being outdoors.

From his upstairs window, Hedley looked down at the street boy and his dog. The boy was lying in a ball in his sleeping bag, with the dog curled up next to him.

Then, one morning, on his way to school, Hedley noticed that the boy wasn't there! The green sleeping bag was lying in a heap at the entrance of the boarded-up store, and the dog was lying on it, whining.

A feeling of panic rushed through Hedley's heart. He knew something was horribly wrong.

At school, Hedley couldn't keep his mind on his schoolwork. He kept wondering what had happened to the street boy. He wouldn't have left his dog there all alone!

On the way home, he stopped at the subway station. His parents had told him to always come directly home, but Hedley couldn't help himself.

The boy still wasn't there. And the dog looked so miserable on its own.

"Where's the boy who's always with that dog?" he asked the newspaperman.

"He's sick," the old man explained. "Gone to the hospital, poor kid."

An awful feeling went through Hedley's body when he heard this.

"When's he coming back?"

"Dunno," the old man replied.

Hedley crossed the road and went indoors. He lay down on his bed, his head aching.

By the time his mother came home from work, he was weak and pale. She called for a doctor, who examined Hedley, then prescribed some medicine.

Hedley's condition worsened during the night, and he spent fitful hours tossing and turning, passing in and out of sleep, tortured by dreams of the street boy in the hospital.

The next day, Hedley was feverish. At times, he seemed to lose consciousness altogether. When he came around, he asked only for sips of water as the thought of food made him nauseous. During the following night, his family was worried about him. He ranted and raved, complaining that they shouldn't have left him out in the snow during such freezing weather. He didn't recognize his mother or father.

For three days, Hedley was delirious. But on the morning of the fourth day, he woke up feeling much better. The dizziness was gone, the nightmares had vanished, and the fever had dropped.

He sat up, but he could hardly believe his eyes!

Where was he?

He was outdoors!

He was shocked to find himself lying on a few sheets of cardboard, huddled inside a dark green sleeping bag.

He recognized the entrance of the boarded-up store. Curled up beside him was a scruffy dog, who wagged its tail joyfully when it saw that Hedley had woken up.

Hedley couldn't figure out what had happened. But here he was, dressed in clothes that were old and shabby, huddled in a sleeping bag, while people walked past without even noticing him.

"Morning, kiddo."

It was the toothless newspaperman.

"You're looking a lot better today," he added cheerfully.

"How did I get here?" Hedley asked.

"The same guy who took you to the hospital brought you back," the old man explained.

Hedley wanted to say he'd never gone to the hospital. But at that moment he noticed his father emerging from the house across the road.

Hedley climbed out of his sleeping bag and rushed to greet him. The dog immediately followed. Hedley had to pick it up, so that they could cross the road safely. He had to wait for a break in the traffic, and by the time Hedley reached his father, he was just getting into the car. Hedley's father deliberately pulled the car door shut and started the engine.

"Dad!" Hedley shouted.

Hedley's father barely looked at him as he drove off.

Hedley was stunned. His father had not recognized him!

He marched up to the front door of his house and rang the doorbell.

His mother came to the door and opened it.

"What do you want?" she asked.

"Mom, don't you know who I am?" Hedley said.

Hedley's mother tried to shut the door, but Hedley put his foot out and prevented it from closing.

"Mom, it's me. Hedley!"

"Don't be ridiculous!" his mother said, looking at him with terror in her eyes. "Hedley's upstairs."

Hedley hardly knew what to say or do.

"Please let me in, Mom!"

"Go away!" his mother screamed. "Leave us alone or I'll call the police."

Hedley backed away. His mother closed the door. He crossed the road back to the subway station. The dog snuggled up against him. He lay there, cold and confused.

A while later, Hedley noticed the curtains being opened in the upstairs room across the road. A boy looked out of the window. Hedley recognized him. It was the street boy! In Hedley's room!

Hedley felt very strange. What was going on?

His stomach was growling with hunger.

"I'm starving," he said to the newspaperman.

"You've forgotten to put out your cap," the old man responded. "But here, you can have this in the meantime."

The old man took out half a sandwich from his pocket.

"Thanks," Hedley said.

Hedley found a cap under his sleeping bag and laid it out in front of him. The morning rush hour had started, but no one dropped any money into Hedley's cap.

The front door of the house across the street opened, and the street boy emerged, dressed for school. He looked so clean! He walked past the station and disappeared around the corner.

The day passed slowly. Eventually, Hedley's cap contained some coins. He bought a bag of chips from the station snack stand and shared it with the dog.

Later in the day, the street boy returned from school. Hedley saw him coming and intercepted him.

"Why are you living in my house?" Hedley asked him.

The street boy looked at Hedley as if he were a dangerous maniac.

"Leave me alone!" the boy said.

"No!" Hedley said firmly. "You stay here with your dog and give me the front door key so I can go home."

The street boy pulled away from Hedley, but Hedley grabbed hold of him and tried to get the key that he knew was in the boy's jacket pocket.

"Stop it!" the street boy shouted.

The two boys started pulling at each other, punching and hitting.

The newspaperman hobbled over and separated them.

"Enough of that, boys!"

The street boy straightened himself up and crossed the road.

"You shouldn't be allowed to live on the streets!" he yelled back, as he let himself in the front door.

That night, Hedley slept outdoors. He huddled in his sleeping bag and hugged the dog for warmth. He thought of going to the police himself to tell them he was the real Hedley. But, of course, they wouldn't believe a boy dressed in shabby clothes.

Hedley found it difficult to sleep on the concrete. It was too cold, for one thing. And uncomfortable. And noisy. The cars going past made a terrific racket. When Hedley finally did fall asleep, he was woken after just a few hours by some drunk men who were passing by. They poured beer all over his sleeping bag, just for a laugh. The men made fun of Hedley and swore at him for a while before staggering off. Hedley didn't sleep much the rest of the night; he was too damp.

The next morning, after the rush hour, Hedley was wondering how to get through the day, when, suddenly, he heard a voice.

"Hey!" the voice. "Let's go to the food kitchen."

Hedley looked to see where the voice was coming from. The only thing nearby was the scruffy dog.

"Well, you comin' or what?"

It was the dog!

Hedley stashed his sleeping bag in a corner of the shop entrance.

"You can talk?" Hedley said.

"Well, no point going on and on about it," the dog said. "Let's get going."

The dog knew the way. He had traveled there every day for months.

At the food kitchen, Hedley stood in a line of street people. All of them had spent their night somewhere on the streets. Some of them looked in really bad condition, coughing and hacking. Others looked like ordinary people, Hedley thought.

Inside the building, Hedley downed a carton of milk and ate some beans on toast. It brought some life back to his aching body. One or two street people spoke to him and asked him where he hung out. But on the whole, he kept to himself.

After the meal, the dog said, "Hey, what about something for me?"

So Hedley asked the person behind the counter if they had any scraps or leftovers.

"Here you are, Mutt," the woman said, offering the

dog some cold french fries and half a burger from the trash can.

Hedley spent the rest of the day begging outside the station. In the afternoon, he spent what he had earned on a secondhand sweater he found in a thrift shop.

One day followed after another. In a story, days can pass as quickly as this, but for Hedley, each day was a long, hard day of real time.

Most people walked past him without a comment. Several older men in suits made nasty comments about boys begging for money from decent people. But often, young people stopped, spoke to him, and gave him money. At night, he grew accustomed to the noise of cars, but still he was woken by cats fighting, radios blasting, or people arguing at three in the morning. One night, he was woken by a flashlight shining into his face. It was the police! They searched his pockets, found nothing, and told him he better find somewhere else to live soon.

The next day, Hedley was tired, bored, and miserable.

"You need to clean yourself up!" the dog said to him. "You're getting dirtier than me."

The dog led Hedley to a shelter for homeless people, where he was given a white robe to change into. He put the clothes he had worn for the last week into a washing machine. Then he took a shower.

Afterward, Mutt said, "You smell a lot better now!"

All the time that he slept near the subway station, Hedley kept an eye on his old home. It was difficult for him to observe his family living their orderly lives, and the boy who used to live on the streets enjoying the warmth of Hedley's bedroom, while Hedley froze out there in the cold.

One evening, Hedley noticed his father struggling to pull something large out of the back of his car. It was a shiny new bike! His father wheeled it to the front of the house and called the boy from upstairs to look at it. Then it dawned on Hedley, who was watching all this with interest. It was his birthday! Of course it was! And Hedley's parents had told him they were going to buy him a bike.

Hedley watched as the boy climbed on the bike. He seemed really pleased with the gift.

Hedley was furious.

He ran across the street and shouted at his parents.

"That bike's mine! It's my birthday today, not his! You're my parents!"

"Get out of here!" Hedley's father shouted. Then he told his wife to go indoors and call the police.

Hedley retreated back to his spot outside the boarded-up shop.

"Uh-oh!" the dog said. "You've got us in trouble now."

Sure enough, later that evening the police arrived.

"You got to move, son!" the policeman said. "You can't sleep here anymore. Find yourself a shelter."

"Can I just sleep here tonight?" Hedley asked. "I'll move in the morning."

"No," the policeman answered. "You have to move now. We've had complaints."

Hedley picked up his sleeping bag. The policeman watched him as he disappeared down the street.

"Where to now?" Hedley wondered.

"I know another good doorway," the dog said. "Follow me! I used to hang out there before you found me."

Hedley followed the dog through the city, turning left, right, then straight, on past City Hall.

The dog led Hedley to a deep doorway that was nicely sheltered from the cold, rain, and wind.

"Thanks, Mutt," Hedley said. "This place will do just fine."

He curled up in the corner nearest the shop door, held Mutt close to him, and thought about the night's events. Eventually, he fell asleep.

It was not long after that, though, when he felt himself being kicked!

"This is my bedroom!" someone was shouting. "You can't sleep here."

Hedley sat up to find a furious man hollering at him. He thought of putting up a fight, but the dog said, "Let's go! I know another place."

He led Hedley to an unoccupied doorway, which wasn't deep enough to keep out the rain. But it would have to do. Hedley covered his sleeping bag with a black trash bag to keep himself and Mutt dry.

The weeks passed. The months passed. In a story, months can pass as quickly as this, but for Hedley, each month was a long, hard month of real time.

Hedley got to know some of the other street people: Farrukh, who was a juggler; Donna, who was pregnant; Dave the Rave, who was into drugs.

Winter turned to spring, spring to summer, summer to autumn. In a story, a year can pass as quickly as this, but for Hedley, the year was a long, hard year of real time. And after autumn, the cold wintry weather returned.

The first snow reminded Hedley of the subway station where he and the dog used to live.

"Let's go check it out, Mutt."

"Good idea," the dog replied.

Hedley and the dog approached the subway station. The shop was still boarded up. Hedley spoke to the toothless newspaperman.

"How you doin'?" Hedley asked.

"Not too bad," the old man answered.

"We're thinking of moving back here for a while," Hedley said. "Think it would be okay?"

"Try it," the old man suggested. "Perhaps they'll make you move again, I don't know."

"We got nothin' to lose," Hedley said.

So they moved back to his old spot.

It was excellent to be back. Hedley kept watch on his old family again. His dad had a new car, he noticed. His little sister, Serena, now had a tricycle of her own that she rode in the yard. The street boy, who had taken Hedley's place, used his fancy bike to ride to school and back every day.

Late one afternoon, Hedley bumped into Dave the Rave. They greeted each other with a tap of the knuckles and stood talking on the sidewalk.

Out of the corner of his eye, Hedley noticed the boy from across the road, the one who lived in Hedley's house, who slept in Hedley's bed, returning from school on the bike that should have been Hedley's.

Suddenly, a car backed out of a side street without looking! An oncoming car had to swerve to avoid it. But now the swerving car was heading straight for the street boy on his bike!

Without hesitation, Hedley dived into the street and pushed the street boy out of the way. The bike and the two boys tumbled onto the pavement. But the car drove past without hitting either of them.

Hedley was lying on the street. His head was aching! He had struck it on the pavement. Blood ran down the side of his face.

"Are you all right?"

Dave the Rave and the street boy were standing over him. They lifted him to his feet.

"Yeah, I'm not too bad."

"Be more careful next time!" the street boy said to him, passing him the bike. Some of the black covering had torn off the seat, but otherwise the bike was in good shape.

Hedley was amazed to have the bike handed over to him!

What's going on? he thought.

The street boy and Dave the Rave walked off. The dog followed behind them. Then the street boy and Dave the Rave parted company. Hedley watched in astonishment as the street boy returned to his spot at the subway station! He got into his green sleeping bag and the dog curled up beside him.

Hedley was dazed!

He thought that if the street boy had gone back to the subway station, perhaps he could try going back home.

So he did.

He wheeled his bike slowly across the road. He walked in through the gate of his house. His mother came running out of the front door.

"Hedley! Are you hurt?"

"No, I'm okay," Hedley answered.

"You've got blood on your face!" Serena said.

Hedley's mother led him indoors and doctored his injury. He went upstairs to wash and change into other clothes. Then he went back into his bedroom. Everything was still the same. It was as if he had never been away!

How warm his bedroom was, and his bed seemed so soft and luxurious with its springy mattress and clean pillows. From the window, he could see snow falling and the street boy huddled up in his green sleeping bag outside the boarded-up shop.

The street boy suddenly noticed Hedley looking at him. For a moment they stared at each other.

It's going to be a cold winter for him, Hedley thought. *I'm going to give him my parka.*

Oh, how sweet and innocent Janine was!

Janine lived in a house with her mother and stepfather. During the day, they were an ordinary family. Janine went to school, her mother worked in a department store, and her stepfather managed an office in the city.

On the weekends, they were so kind to her, buying her as many sweets as she wanted. Anyone seeing them together in the park or at the mall or on the beach might have thought they were the happiest family in the world.

But Janine lived in a house with a secret room, a room with glass walls. That room was secret from the world outside. No one in the whole wide world knew about that room except for Janine and her mother and stepfather. From that room you could not see out, but from Janine's room, she could see in.

And what things Janine saw each night!

She saw the magician, the wicked magician with a black mustache, dressed in his black suit, top hat, bow tie, and white gloves, pulling a shining silvery sword from the air. She saw his assistant, the beautiful Cosmo, dressed in sparkling tights, high-heel shoes, and a starry, sequined, tight-fitting pink jacket, twirling around in time to the music that was playing.

"Who is tonight's little volunteer?" the magician asked.

"Tonight it's this pretty girl with the blue eyes," the assistant would answer, lifting a veil from the girl who trembled with fear.

She was wearing a sleeveless white dress, her hair braided with ribbons, her cheeks reddened with stage makeup.

"And what's your name, my dear?" the magician asked.

"C . . . C . . . Carolette," the girl stammered.

"Carolette, what a lovely name," the wicked magician said, twisting his black mustache. "Thank you, Cosmo. You may go now. Come back when I ring my golden bell!"

The beautiful Cosmo pirouetted out of the glass room and closed the door behind her.

"Now, Carolette," the magician said. "Let's lay you in this box."

He helped Carolette climb into a long black box.

"Now I'll close the lid," he said. "You're not afraid of the dark, are you, my dear?"

Janine watched as the wicked magician raised his shining silvery sword above his head.

"Watch carefully now," the magician said, "as I perform a trick that has rarely been seen. I will cut the lovely Carolette into small pieces."

The wicked magician brought down the sword sharply and cut through the box that Carolette was lying in.

"Look," he said. "The box is now in two pieces."

He pulled the two pieces of the box apart to show that they really were not joined.

"Watch carefully," he said as he brought down the sword again and again and again.

The long black box was now in five pieces, each small enough for the magician to lift into the air and hold as he marched around in time to the music.

"Here is one leg," he said, holding up one small piece of the box, and, sure enough, there was Carolette's lovely leg.

"And here is the other," he said, and, sure enough, there it was.

"And here is one arm," he said, and, sure enough, there was Carolette's lovely arm.

"And here is the other," he said, and, sure enough, there it was.

"And finally," he said, "here is Carolette's head."

He lifted the piece of the box high above his head, turned around twice, then opened it to reveal Carolette's head.

Carolette's mouth was still talking!

"Please," she whimpered, "don't hurt me!"

"I won't hurt you, my dear," the wicked magician said. "In fact, I'm going to put you all together again, good as new."

He threw his sword up in the air, and it vanished in a puff of smoke.

Then he pulled a magic wand from the air.

"Now, as I utter the magic words, Carolette's arms and legs and head will join together. Just watch carefully."

The magician concentrated on the five pieces of the box that lay before him.

He pushed these pieces together until they all touched one another.

"Al jehurra kenassi beshurra kedal!" the wicked magician chanted.

He lifted the lid and Carolette sat up.

"Are you all in one piece?" the magician asked.

Carolette stepped out of the box.

"Good. I'm sure you enjoyed that," the magician said. "But you must never tell anyone in the whole wide world what went on here tonight, because this is the most secret magic there is."

Then the magician picked up the golden bell and rang it loud and clear.

Cosmo, the assistant, came dancing in through the door of the glass room.

"The show is over for tonight," the magician announced. "Well done, Carolette. Do a curtsy!"

And Carolette had to curtsy. The magician and Cosmo clapped their hands.

"You can take Carolette back now," the magician said to his assistant.

Cosmo wrapped a veil around Carolette and led her out of the glass room.

Night after night, Janine watched the magic show. It made her flesh creep to see the wicked magician cut the lovely Carolette into five pieces.

One day, she told herself, *I'm going to rescue Carolette from the wicked magician.*

But she didn't know how to do it.

The show was always the same, night after night. The sweet Carolette was chopped into five pieces and then put back again. Always the same costumes, always the same music, always the same magic chant, *"Al jehurra kenassi beshurra kedal!"*

But one night, the wicked magician chopped the black box into five pieces, and when he showed what was in each piece — the two arms, the two legs, the head of Carolette with the mouth whimpering, "Please don't hurt me!" — each of the pieces was bleeding!

Blood was smeared all over the sweet Carolette's arms and legs and head!

Janine couldn't bear it! She screamed and screamed and screamed!

Then the wicked magician pushed the pieces of the box together. He chanted, *"Al jehurra kenassi beshurra kedal!"* And Carolette sat up as good as new, all in one piece, sparkling clean. No trace of blood anywhere!

"Wasn't that the most brilliant magic trick you've ever seen?" the wicked magician asked.

He rang the golden bell, and when Cosmo came into the glass room, she and the magician clapped and shouted, "Bravo! Bravo!"

But that night, after the show, Janine couldn't sleep a wink. The next morning, when she got to school, she couldn't sit still in class, so she ran to the playground. Beyond the playground was the footpath leading down to the woods. It was forbidden to go beyond the playground into those woods.

But Janine opened the gate and ran through. Tears were streaming down her face. She ran on and on to the middle of the woods, not caring where she was heading. Then she stopped and leaned against the trunk of an old tree.

She wept and wept, and then she blurted out the secret she was never supposed to tell anyone in the whole wide world.

"The wicked magician made Carolette bleed!" she

screamed. "The wicked magician chopped Carolette into five pieces and made her bleed!"

Unseen by Janine, a glistening black raven, sitting at the top of the tree, heard her words.

Immediately, it flew off over the woods, screeching, "The wicked magician made Carolette bleed!"

Toward the school it flew, screeching, "The wicked magician chopped Carolette into five pieces and made her bleed!"

Janine slumped down to the bottom of the trunk and sobbed. She wished she didn't have to go back home. She wished she could disappear from the world. She wished she could forget everything that had happened night after night.

Suddenly, Janine felt hands on her shoulders. They were gently trying to comfort her.

"Janine? Janine? Are you all right?"

It was her teacher, Miss Gresham.

Janine sobbed uncontrollably.

"My poor dear," Miss Gresham said soothingly. "We must do something about that wicked magician. I know someone who can help."

That night, just as the show in the glass room was about to begin — Cosmo, the assistant, was twirling around in her sequined jacket, and the wicked magician was pulling his shining silvery sword from the air — just then, while Carolette stood trembling under her veil, there was an urgent banging on the door. Then she heard the sound of wood shattering.

White smoke filled the glass room, followed by a flash of brilliant light. Out of nowhere, there stood before them a white-bearded wizard, holding a staff that was crackling with little flames.

"I am the Great Marquez!" he announced. "One move, and you will be sizzled to ashes!"

The wicked magician and Cosmo looked petrified.

Carolette shuffled closer to the Great Marquez.

"I have come to put an end to this show!" he said in his great booming voice. He stared at the wicked magician so fiercely that the magician had to turn his head away. "Never again will you perform your wicked magic!"

The Great Marquez banged three times on the floor with his staff. And each time a slash of lightning blinded everyone in the room.

Then the Great Marquez stepped across to the wicked magician, grabbed hold of his shining silvery sword, and broke it in half. He put the golden bell on the floor and stamped it flat so that it could never ring again. He pulled off the wicked magician's top hat, bow tie, and gloves, squeezing them until they turned to ashes. Then the Great Marquez ripped off the wicked magician's mustache! The wicked magician slumped to the floor.

And, suddenly, the wicked magician didn't look like a magician any longer. He looked like Janine's stepfather!

The Great Marquez turned to Cosmo, the assistant, and banged again three times on the floor with his staff. Again, the lightning flashed. This time, a robe appeared in his hands, which he wrapped around Cosmo.

And, suddenly, she didn't look like a wicked magician's assistant any longer. She looked like Janine's mother! And she was sobbing, crying, "I'm so sorry! I'm so sorry!"

Finally, the Great Marquez turned to Carolette. Once more, he banged on the floor three times with his staff. Lightning flashed in all directions.

He took a handkerchief from his pocket and wiped the red stage makeup from her face.

Suddenly, she didn't look like Carolette any longer. She looked like Janine!

"Never again will you have to pretend to be Carolette," he said tenderly to her.

Then the Great Marquez faced Janine's stepfather. "Your wicked magic has come to an end," he boomed. "The show is over. This glass room is secret no longer."

He banged three times on the floor with his staff. The glass windows of the little room immediately began to melt. They melted into pools of liquid on the floor, which then evaporated into wisps of steam.

Nothing was left of the secret room.

"And now," the Great Marquez said, "I give to this girl Janine the gift of sleep during the night and during the day the power to grow and to understand herself and others. She will see her parents for who they truly are. And from this day forth, I will be watching over her to keep her safe."

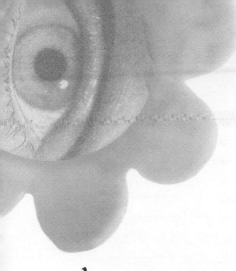

If you've heard this story before, then you've heard more than I have, because I've never heard it before and I've heard most stories.

It happened in a city that was just like any other city, except that everything painted blue in other cities was painted red in this one. And it happened in a time that was just like now. Except that it was then.

In this city, there lived a girl called Megan. She was a lovely and cheerful girl, with hair the color of milk chocolate and a smile that lit up the neighborhood.

Now, Megan was approaching a marriageable age. Young men swarmed around, howling like wild dogs.

"Megan, please marry me!" one would say, showing off the mountainous muscles on his upper arms.

"No, marry me!" insisted another, inviting her to ride in his gleaming sports car.

"It would be a great mistake to marry anyone other

than myself!" said a third, combing his greased-back hair and posing like a film star.

But Megan would have none of them, until one day a soft-spoken young man named Conrad Avery was introduced to her.

How interesting Conrad seemed to her! How easily they spoke together, talking about this and that. He was gentle and a little nervous, but he became more confident as his affection toward Megan blossomed into love.

After a while, he showed Megan a photograph of his family, a photograph he kept in his wallet at all times. He spoke so tenderly of his parents, his grandparents, and his great-aunt. It made Megan feel warm toward Conrad to think how much of a family man he was.

He is the one for me, Megan thought to herself. *He loves me and I love him. He will be a caring father to our children.*

When, after some months, he proposed marriage, she accepted.

But the day after her wedding, Megan was in for a big surprise.

They woke up the next morning and Conrad said, "Good morning, dear wife! An apple a day keeps the doctor away!"

"Good morning, dear husband," Megan said. "What's this about apples?"

"Don't you know," he replied, "that when we wake up

you must say, 'An apple a day keeps the doctor away!' otherwise the day won't go well?"

"Very well." She laughed. "An apple a day keeps the doctor away!"

Conrad washed and dressed, then helped cook breakfast. But before sitting down, he placed the newspaper on top of his head and said, "Merrily we roll along."

"What's this 'merrily we roll along' business?" his wife asked.

"Don't you know," her husband replied, "that before eating you must always do and say this, otherwise the food will taste like manure?"

"Very well." Megan laughed. And she placed a newspaper on her head and said, "Merrily we roll along."

After breakfast, they both put on their coats and walked to the car to drive to work.

But before he climbed in, Conrad walked around the car three times, and each time he said, "May the heavens swallow up all fish crabs!"

"What's all this?" Megan asked.

"Don't you know," Conrad said, "that you must do this before getting into a car, otherwise you will never reach your destination?"

"Is this really necessary?" Megan asked.

"Indeed it is!" Conrad said. "Please, Megan. Otherwise, I'll never get to work safely!"

Out of love for her husband, Megan circled the car three times, and each time she repeated, "May the heavens swallow up all fish crabs!"

That evening, when he finished his work at the post office, Conrad picked up his wife from the bank where she worked. He kissed her sweetly on the cheek and they drove home like any two newlyweds in love, glad to be together.

Conrad parked the car in the driveway, then unlocked the front door. He stepped into the house with his right foot, then stepped out of it with his left, three times in a row, each time accompanying the action with the words "toosh-aloosh." Only when this was completed correctly did he go indoors.

"What's this 'toosh-aloosh' business?" Megan asked.

"Don't you know," Conrad replied, "that you must step in and out of the house three times and say 'toosh-aloosh' before going in, otherwise there will be no happiness in our home?"

So Megan said, "toosh-aloosh," while stepping in and out of the house three times.

After dinner, before he could do the dishes, Conrad touched the taps, counting to twenty-one. But he didn't count in the usual way. Instead, he counted, "one, two, three . . . two, three, four . . . three, four, five . . . four, five, six . . ." and so on, so that it took a lot longer than it would have if he simply counted in the usual way.

"What's all this counting for?" Megan asked.

"Don't you know," Conrad replied, "that if you don't count to twenty-one in this exact way, your children will never grow up healthy, wealthy, and wise?"

So Megan was forced to touch the taps and count.

"One, two, three . . ." she said. "Two, three, four . . . three, four, five . . . four, five, six . . ." all the way to twenty-one.

After doing the dishes, they spent several delightful hours in each other's company. Megan really loved Conrad and he loved her, too.

When it was time to go to sleep, Conrad brushed his teeth, changed into his pajamas, then climbed into bed.

After a brief silence, he curled into a small ball and mumbled, "Sheep in the meadow, cows in the corn."

Then he straightened himself out and smiled at Megan.

"What's this 'sheep and cows' business?" she asked him.

"Don't you know," he said, "that the stars will fall on our house unless we say this?"

So Megan curled herself into a small ball and mumbled, "Sheep in the meadow, cows in the corn."

Then she straightened herself and kissed her husband good night.

The next morning when Megan awoke, she thought of pleasing Conrad, so she turned to him and said, "Good morning, dear husband! An apple a day keeps the doctor away!"

Conrad jumped out of bed, fretting and fuming. He went into the bathroom and washed his hands twenty-four times, each time repeating, "Forget the walruses! Forgive the warthogs!"

"What did I do wrong?" she asked anxiously.

"Don't you know," he said, "that today is Tuesday? On Tuesdays you must say 'An orange a day keeps the dentist away!'"

Poor Megan!

She soon learned that everything was slightly different on Tuesdays, different again on Wednesdays, Thursdays, Fridays, and completely different on Saturdays and Sundays!

It took her a long time to learn all the words and actions for each different day and occasion.

And that was just the tip of the iceberg!

Over the next few months, Megan learned that Conrad made her perform only the most necessary actions. There were hundreds of others, which were less important, that Conrad himself was compelled to perform: tying shoelaces, opening cupboards, feeding the cat — all these had to be repeated until done correctly, with the appropriate words, otherwise Conrad felt things would not go well for him and his wife. And on the first day of each month all these had to be done backward!

But Megan loved Conrad, so she tried her best to help her husband through each day.

After a year, she noticed that other actions were being added to the list. And the actions were becoming more and more complicated! For example, after dinner, they had to count to larger and larger numbers, first to thirty-one, forty-one, fifty-one, then right up to one hundred and one. "One, two, three . . . two, three, four . . . three, four, five . . . four, five, six . . ." all the way up to one hundred and one!

One day, they were shopping at the supermarket. They had bought everything they needed and Conrad took out his wallet to pay the cashier. When he received the receipt, he jumped up and down three times and said, "Forever's a long time to fill with pigeons!"

He pushed the shopping cart out the automatic door. As they neared the car, he stopped, put his fingers in his ears, and shouted, "Gateway to the stars!"

Megan was so embarrassed! It was the first time Conrad had acted like this in public. But Megan simply held his hand and reassured him. "It's all right, darling," she said.

Later, after they had put the groceries in the car, Megan pushed the cart back to the store.

Suddenly, she felt a tap on her shoulder. She turned around to see a most unusual-looking person. He was short and plump with a purple face, a long yellow beard, curly yellow hair, and enormous feet.

"Excuse me, lady," he said. "But I couldn't help noticing your husband earlier. . . ."

"It's none of your business," she said.

"That's true," the man answered. "But I may be able to help. . . ."

"How can you help . . . ?"

"Your husband's under a spell," the man continued, "and I'm a Nonnigon."

"What's that?" Megan asked.

"Nonnigons are brilliant spellbreakers," he explained.

The man fished in his pocket and pulled out a small business card.

"If you ever need me, give me a call." And with that the man was gone, flapping his enormous feet as he walked off.

Megan looked at the card. There, in gold letters, were printed the words: SPELLBREAKER FRIDAFROTH. But the rest of the card, including the back, was blank. There was no number to call!

That's not much use! Megan thought, slipping the card into her purse.

In time, she forgot about the card, but she did begin to wonder if her husband was indeed under a spell. Every minute of every day was taken up with ridiculous actions. There was hardly a moment for anything else! And how complicated all the actions were. After dinner now, they both had to touch the taps and count to five hundred and one! It took so long! "One, two, three . . . two, three, four . . . three, four, five . . . four, five, six . . ." all the way up to five hundred and one!

After two years of marriage, Megan was becoming very unhappy. It was upsetting to watch her husband's life — and her own — being swallowed up by all these actions. But what bothered her more than anything else was the fact that she wanted to have a baby. How could she with all this going on?

If I ever had a child, she thought, *it would also have to live under this terrible spell. It would have to learn all these words and actions! Never, never, never!*

She went upstairs to the bedroom, shut the door, and wept and wept.

Oh, if only that Nonnigon had left me his number, she thought. *Perhaps he might have been able to break the spell.*

She searched her purse for the card. There it was: SPELLBREAKER FRIDAFROTH.

What could she do to find him? Tears rolled down her cheeks and dripped onto the blank card.

To her astonishment, letters began to form where the tears fell. Light yellow letters, but visible enough to read: NEED HELP? CALL 555-5920.

Megan picked up the telephone and dialed.

"Institute of Spellbreaking," the voice on the other end answered. "Yes, you can have an appointment with Fridafroth but there's a long waiting list. The earliest appointment is in three months." The voice gave her a time and date.

Later in the day, Megan told Conrad about the phone call. But he didn't want to hear about it. He didn't want to keep the appointment. He agreed he might be under a spell, but if he went to a spellbreaker, he might have to stop doing these things. Then something bad might happen to them!

Megan, however, was insistent. If he loved her, she said, he'd come with her to the spellbreaker.

"All right," he agreed. "But don't expect me to change my ways!"

As the weeks passed and the day of the appointment approached, Conrad became increasingly nervous. But he didn't want to disappoint Megan.

The Institute of Spellbreaking was in a new part of the city that Megan and Conrad had never seen before. The buildings were all of unusual shapes and colors. Megan and Conrad eventually located the institute itself, a curved building with an imposing entrance flanked by tall pillars.

"I can't go in there!" Conrad screamed. "I can't, Megan! I'm sorry, I just can't!"

He turned and ran down the street as fast as he could. But he didn't get that far, because the road ended abruptly at the river, where a large ferryboat, loaded with cars and passengers, was heading to the other side of the river.

Megan walked in the direction Conrad had gone and found him at the river's edge, in a state of panic.

"Forget the worms! Forgive the woodpeckers!"

"Dear Conrad," she said tenderly. "Put your hand here!" She placed Conrad's hand on her stomach.

"What is it?" he asked her.

"Can't you feel?" she said. "Can't you feel any kicking?"

Conrad's hand felt little movements coming from inside Megan's stomach.

"It's our baby, Conrad," Megan said. "I'm pregnant!"

Conrad stared at her. Gradually, he calmed down and began to smile as a feeling of joy came over him.

"I'm going to be a father!" he yelped, clapping his hands and jumping around.

"Yes, Conrad. And you can do something right now for your baby. You can come and see the spellbreaker."

"Yes, dear. Of course."

Arm in arm, Conrad and Megan entered the institute. The interior of the building was sparsely furnished. They had to walk down a long hallway to reach the reception desk.

"Yes, and who have we here?"

The words came from a short and plump, yellow-bearded, curly-haired Nonnigon, sitting on a tall stool. He asked for their names.

"Fridafroth will see you shortly," the receptionist said. "Please take a seat."

They sat anxiously in the waiting area. From time to time, various Nonnigons scurried from one side of the building to the other, their large feet flapping on the floor with each step.

After a long wait, Megan recognized the one coming toward them.

"Mrs. Avery, how good to see you again. And you, sir," Fridafroth said, extending a hand toward Conrad. "I apologize for keeping you waiting. Busy day. People are under such stress and strain nowadays. Spellbound in more ways than you can possibly imagine."

He led them to his consulting room, which was furnished with a desk, three chairs, and floor-to-ceiling shelves laden with numerous bottles and books. There were also several potted plants scattered around the room, some of them with spiky stems, hairy leaves, and bell-like blooms.

"Take a seat, please."

Nonnigon Fridafroth spent an hour talking to Megan and Conrad, learning about each word and action that they were compelled to repeat during any one day.

"Aha! An orange a day . . ." he said, gazing at them

over his glasses. "Oho! Toosh-aloosh . . . mmmhmm, walruses and warthogs . . . I think I'm getting the picture."

"Can you help us, Mr. Fridafroth?" Megan asked.

"Only with your cooperation, Mr. Avery."

"Certainly, Mr. Fridafroth."

"Please stand in front of the mirror."

Neither Conrad nor Megan had noticed the full-length mirror until then. They had never seen one like it before. It was made of black glass.

"Now, who do you see in that mirror? Look closely, Mr. Avery."

Conrad stared at his image.

"It's me, of course," he replied.

"Keep looking!" Nonnigon Fridafroth insisted. "Don't turn away."

Conrad fixed his gaze on the mirror.

"Good heavens!" he exclaimed suddenly. "That's my great-aunt staring back at me!"

"Your great-aunt!" Nonnigon Fridafroth repeated. "So, it was she who cast the spell!"

Conrad was bewildered.

"You can sit down now, Mr. Avery."

Megan patted Conrad's arm gently.

"What we need to do now," Nonnigon Fridafroth continued, "is to break the power she has over you."

"How can we do that?" Conrad asked.

"Can you tell me more about her? Describe her to me," Nonnigon Fridafroth said.

"She was. . . . She was . . ." Conrad tried to think of what to say.

"Show your photograph," Megan suggested.

"Which photograph is that?" Nonnigon Fridafroth asked.

"He keeps a family photograph in his wallet," Megan explained.

Conrad anxiously took the photo from the wallet.

"May I see it?" Nonnigon Fridafroth requested, holding out his hand.

"No!" Conrad exclaimed, clutching the photo tightly. "I have never let anyone else hold it."

Megan turned sweetly to her husband, who furrowed his brow and scowled.

"Come now, dear," she implored.

"Forget the wolves! Forgive the weasels!" Conrad cried as he placed the photograph in the Nonnigon's hands. "My great-aunt is the one in the top corner of the picture."

Nonnigon Fridafroth examined the photograph closely.

Then, suddenly, he pointed at Conrad's left hand.

"Whose ring is that?" he asked, pointing at the broad gold band on Conrad's fourth finger.

"It's mine!" Conrad said.

"Yes, but who gave it to you?"

"Somebody when I was twelve . . ." Conrad said.

"Yes, yes," Nonnigon Fridafroth said. "But who gave it to you?"

Conrad pursed his lips and looked around as if he were searching for a way out.

"My . . . my . . . my great-aunt!"

"Conrad," Megan said gently. "I never knew that."

"Give it to me!" Nonnigon Fridafroth said.

"I can't," Conrad answered.

"Why not?"

"Because it won't come off my finger."

Conrad pulled on it to show how the ring refused to budge. His finger was much bigger now than when he first put it on all those years ago.

Nonnigon Fridafroth rose from his chair and consulted a book that was so thick it looked as though it weighed more than himself.

"Aha . . . oho . . . mmmhmmm . . ." he muttered as he browsed through the information contained in those weighty pages.

Then he started pouring substances from bottles into a glass beaker that he heated on a gas burner. It gurgled and gargled! He plucked a crimson flower from one of the potted plants near his desk, then carefully tore it into small pieces that he added to the brew. It sputtered and splattered! A thick crimson smoke rose up to the ceiling and a powerful odor pervaded the room. Finally, he took the photograph of Conrad's family and held the top corner of it in the crimson smoke with a long pair of tweezers.

Conrad broke into a dreadful sobbing.

"Forget the wasps! Forgive the weevils!"

"There, there, my dear," Megan said, comforting her husband by putting her arm around his shoulders.

After a while, Nonnigon Fridafroth returned the photograph to Conrad.

"I have treated it with spellbreaking vapors," he explained. "Now the ring will come off easily."

Conrad pulled on the ring, and it slid off without any difficulty.

"You can keep the photograph," the Nonnigon said. "But you need to be freed from the power of this ring."

He walked across to the gas burner and dropped the gold ring into the sizzling mixture.

It fizzed and whizzed, slowly dissolving until it was no thicker than a fine wire. Then it broke in two and dissolved further until it completely vanished.

Conrad broke into a dreadful sobbing.

"Forget the weasels! Forgive the wombats!"

Nonnigon Fridafroth continued his brewing. He allowed the mixture to boil for a while, after which he poured the crimson liquid into a large bottle.

"Now, Mr. Avery, what I'd like you to do is to think of

one of your rituals and write the words that you say on this piece of paper. Choose carefully which you'd like to get rid of first."

Conrad thought for a moment, then wrote, *An apple a day keeps the doctor away.*

"Very good, Mr. Avery. Now I'd like you to drop the piece of paper in the bottle."

Conrad did as he was asked. The liquid sizzled and fizzled. Crimson vapors issued from the bottle as the piece of paper dissolved and disappeared entirely.

"Excellent! Excellent! I don't think that one will give you any trouble tomorrow," Nonnigon Fridafroth exclaimed. "I would like you to take this bottle home with you. Each day, write the words of a different ritual on a piece of paper and drop it in. Every time you do that it will make the spell weaker. After a few months, you'll be much happier and the power of the spell will be broken forever."

"Thank you very much, Mr. Fridafroth," Megan said as she and her husband left.

"My pleasure, my pleasure!" the Nonnigon said, waving good-bye.

The following morning, Conrad awoke and did not mention any fruit. Instead, he turned to Megan and said, "Good morning, dear wife! I have a feeling this day is going to go very well."

Megan was overjoyed.

"Why don't you sizzle another one of your rituals right now?"

Conrad agreed. He wrote, *Merrily we roll along,* on a piece of paper and dropped it into the bottle. Again, crimson vapors spiraled from the bottle as the piece of paper dissolved and disappeared entirely.

When Conrad sat down to breakfast he did not put the newspaper on his head, nor did the food taste like manure.

"This breakfast is delicious!" he said to Megan.

The following day, Conrad sizzled the words, *May the heavens swallow up all fish crabs.* When it was time to go to work, he did not mention fish crabs, nor did he walk around the car three times. He and Megan climbed into the car, drove off, and reached their destinations safely.

Oh, what relief Megan and Conrad felt! It was as if a huge and heavy metal coat had been removed from both of them and they could now move freely, stretching their arms and dancing to the happy music of their lives.

Some months later, a lovely baby daughter was born to the happy couple. What proud parents they were! And the baby grew up free from the spell that had imprisoned her father.

You may be wondering if Conrad was totally freed from his spell. The answer, I'm pleased to tell you, is yes.

Except for one thing. Every twenty-ninth day of February, Conrad would greet his wife first thing in the morning with, "A peach a day keeps the nurse away!"

And because that only occurred once every four years, it didn't cause too much of a problem!

Barnaby Gribb was the most famous scientist of his generation, though to most people who knew him in his early days, he looked perfectly ordinary. He didn't wear a white lab coat, he didn't have wild, white hair, and he didn't wear thick-lensed glasses.

Most people who knew him thought highly of him. They could never have guessed what would befall him.

It's important to realize that Barnaby was very, very, very, very intelligent. Please note: That's four "very"s. Three "very"s wouldn't adequately describe him at all. When it came to intelligence, Barnaby was definitely a "four-very" man. He had been a professor of astrobio-physiology at the university since the age of thirteen, though he was required to teach there only one day each year. The rest of the time he spent in his laboratory that he had built at great expense on the summit of the tallest hill in the city.

He had been married once to a beautiful chemist he

met at a scientific conference. But after giving birth to a baby daughter, his young wife fell in love with a pop star and flew off with him to California. Barnaby was left with the baby, Kaylie, whom he loved more than anything else in the world. He hired a nanny to take care of her while he was busy doing his research, which was most of the time.

Barnaby allowed himself three breaks per day: at eleven o'clock in the morning, four o'clock in the afternoon, and nine o'clock at night. His assistant, a snazzily dressed young man named John Feather, served him snacks and food in the laboratory. During these breaks, Barnaby loved to sit in his old wicker chair, munching his food and solving any problems that randomly occurred to him.

It was at these moments that he made some of his most remarkable breakthroughs, like finding the first black hole in America, which everyone now knows is in Baltimore, and the discovery of nizzles, those microscopic creatures that cause people to sneeze exactly when they do.

Meanwhile, Kaylie grew into a charming young girl. She was proud of her father, though during the week she saw him only at bedtimes when he always read her a scientific article to help her fall asleep. On the weekends, however, they had good times together, and Barnaby was grateful to have the company of such a sweet daughter.

Perhaps their happiness could have continued if not for Barnaby's overwhelming desire to become the most famous scientist of all time. It was this ambition that led him deeper and deeper into forbidden areas of research. It was his belief that the human brain used only ten percent of its potential. He, therefore, began to experiment with the components of life-energy itself, in the hope of producing a substance that would reach those parts of the brain that other substances failed to reach.

Day after day, year after year, Barnaby experimented with various potions that increased intelligence or mental power, prevented the onset of baldness, or enabled humans to live longer. His laboratory filled with an alarming collection of fungi, sea creatures, and the internal organs of seals, orangutans, and turtles.

The closer he came to his goal, the more excited Barnaby became.

One morning, during his break, he exploded with joy.

"My dear Feather!" he exclaimed. "I believe I have done it! A substance that will give me superhuman powers and everlasting fame!"

During his afternoon break, Barnaby worked out most of the formula. During the evening break, he had almost solved the problem of how to manufacture the product.

The exact ingredients in Professor Gribb's formula cannot be revealed, for fear that you might try to produce it yourself and then the awful things that happened to the professor might happen to you. But it involved the skins of certain frogs, the horn of a rhinoceros, nitroglycerine, cobra venom, the liver of a shark, the juice of a nettle, and the tail of a rat.

But there was still something lacking in his formula. As he sat in his old wicker chair late that night, he felt uneasy.

"It needs an extra something," he said to himself as he dozed off for a few moments. "Something potent . . ."

"Perhaps I can help you," he heard a voice say.

The professor sat up in a state of dazed surprise. There, on the end of his desk, wrapped in a mantle of flames, perched a small being. Its eyes were completely white, its ears resembled bat's wings. Its skin consisted of thousands of tiny fishlike scales, and its hands and feet were clawed like a bird's.

"Who are you?" the professor asked.

"Why, surely you recognize me," the little creature said. "I've been your inspiration all these years. The one who has given you all your best ideas."

"Oh, yes," Barnaby said. "I've just never met you in person before."

"Well, I thought I had better come in the flesh, so to speak, because you need a little inspiration tonight."

"That's true," Professor Gribb said. "I just can't figure out the missing ingredient . . ."

"That's because you're thinking you need something

potent," the little creature said. "But in truth, you need something pure and innocent."

"Pure and innocent? What are you talking about?"

"I'm talking about something soft and golden."

"Soft and golden? Can't you be more specific?"

"Yes, Professor, I can. I'm referring to your daughter's hair."

"Kaylie's hair?"

"Yes," the creature explained. "Her hair is the missing ingredient."

"Oh, well. She won't miss one or two hairs from her head."

"That wouldn't be enough."

"A lock of hair, then. Will that do?"

"No! What is required is all her hair!"

"All of it!" Barnaby cried out. "But then she'd be bald!"

"Bald as an egg, Professor. But you'll go down in history as the inventor of the most powerful substance ever known on Earth, mark my words!"

Barnaby Gribb pondered the situation.

"Oh, all right!" he said. "It will all grow back in time, I expect."

The little creature beamed.

"You're a true man of science, Professor Gribb. And I wish you the success you deserve."

The creature hopped off the bed and flew toward the open window.

"It's been a pleasure, Professor Gribb."

And with that, he soared off into the night sky, his mantle of flames glowing fainter and fainter in the distance.

Barnaby roused himself from his bed. Armed with a large pair of scissors, he entered his daughter's bedroom. How sweetly she slept!

Barnaby raised the scissors to his daughter's hair.

"No, I can't do it!" he said. "I can't, I can't, I can't, I can't, I can't, I can't . . . I can!"

And then he snipped off every hair from his daughter's head!

He rushed back to his laboratory with an armful of soft, flowing, golden locks.

He put his daughter's hair into a pot of boiling black syrup. It bubbled into a golden froth.

Professor Gribb worked all night. The pot with the golden froth was still boiling in the morning when John Feather turned up for work.

"Am I not the cleverest man on Earth, Feather? And is this not my greatest achievement?"

John Feather helped Professor Gribb add the remainder of the ingredients. The liquid was then passed through spiral tubes into thick-walled chambers where laser beams flashed violet and green. After this, it was blended in a revolving tub that looked like a washing machine.

"I have decided to call this substance *satanium*,"

Barnaby announced, "In honor of a little visitor I had last night."

"A fine name!" John Feather agreed.

It was at this moment that Kaylie came rushing into the laboratory, weeping miserably.

"Daddy, Daddy!" she cried. "Look what happened to me during the night!"

"Oh, you poor thing!" Professor Gribb said soothingly, hugging her close. "You're as bald as an egg. But don't worry, I still love you."

"But how did it happen, Daddy?"

"I've no idea!" Professor Gribb said, lying through his teeth. "But hurry up now, or you'll be late for school."

"I can't go to school like this!" Kaylie sobbed. "Everyone will laugh at me."

"Oh, very well, then," Barnaby said. "Take a few days off until it grows back."

Kaylie ran back to her room, wailing at the disaster that had befallen her.

That very afternoon, the first drops of satanium were finally distilled into a small test tube. It was a victorious moment for Barnaby Gribb.

"Professor, you are a genius!" John Feather said, congratulating him with a vigorous handshake.

"I completely agree with you, Feather," Professor Gribb replied.

When enough satanium had been produced to fill a

test tube, it was plugged with a leakproof cork that the professor had invented specifically for the satanium. The professor held it up to the light. The liquid was almost transparent, but tinged with gold.

"Beautiful!" he exclaimed.

The satanium tests were conducted scientifically. John Feather had to swear an oath to Professor Gribb that he would never, under any circumstances, divulge any of the results to the outside world. First, they tried it on a model airplane. One drop of satanium was placed in its fuel tank.

"Here we go!" Professor Gribb shouted.

He launched the plane and it soared into the air. Within seconds it disappeared from sight.

"Wow!" John Feather exclaimed. "That's power!"

A week later, the model plane was recovered in Antarctica, where a scientist had observed it running out of energy and floating down to a perfect landing on the ice.

"What do you think of that, Feather?" Professor Gribb asked his assistant.

"It's incredible," the assistant replied.

"Tomorrow we'll try it on the cat!" Professor Gribb announced.

The cat was Jessica, an old Siamese that slept twenty-three hours out of every twenty-four.

One drop of satanium was placed on Jessica's tongue.

She leaped into the air, her hair standing on end, her tail sticking straight up, her eyes bulging and glowing orange, and a vicious meowing issuing from her mouth. She bounded across the laboratory, out through a window, across the garden, and headed straight for the professor's huge German shepherd dog. Claws outstretched, she flew like a missile at the dog's face, as if she were taking out the vengeance of all cats on all dogs. The German shepherd fled for its life, howling in agony. Next, Jessica dashed through the garden gate out into the fields beyond. From the laboratory window, Professor Gribb and John Feather watched in amazement as the revitalized cat sped through the long grass and disappeared into the distance.

That evening, the newspapers were full of stories of a wild beast that had attacked chickens, geese, sheep, and even babies in their strollers. It was past midnight before Jessica returned to Professor Gribb's house. She sidled in and fell asleep in her usual place on the arm of the couch, as if nothing unusual had happened to her all day. She slept most of the day, only waking up to eat and use the litter box.

"Now," Professor Gribb announced, "it is time to test the satanium on myself!"

"Are you sure?" John Feather asked.

"I have never been more sure of anything in my life!" The professor asked his assistant to make notes of everything he did while under the influence of satanium. He also provided instructions that were to be carried out to the last detail if anything went wrong.

Cautiously, John Feather placed one drop of satanium on the professor's outstretched tongue.

Almost immediately, the professor's eyes began to glow with a golden light. His head swelled up to three times its normal size!

"You stupid idiot!" he screamed at John Feather. "What are you looking at? A worm like you has no right to come into my presence without being requested."

"But, Professor," John Feather said. "You were the one who asked me to . . ."

"Get out of here, you sniveling imbecile!" Professor Gribb screamed. "Before I tear you apart for having blue eyes! Blue-eyed dimwits should all be exterminated from the world!"

John Feather backed away from the professor and hid behind a metal cupboard.

Professor Gribb raised his arms until they were stretched out in front of him, and from the fingers of each hand, blue bolts of electric energy flashed across the room, reducing the cupboard instantly to a pile of smoldering metal.

John Feather hurried out of the laboratory, through the front door, and down the steep road.

Professor Gribb followed. But his attention was drawn to other things that appeared to annoy him intensely.

"I've told them for years that no cars should be parked on this street!"

He raised his arms and several blue flashes later there was a neat row of ash piles where each of the cars had once stood.

He continued to walk down the street. Well, actually he didn't walk. It was too fast to be called walking. In fact, it was too fast to be called running. It was an almost instantaneous movement from one place to another. No sooner had he thought of where he'd like to be than he reached it.

Halfway to the center of the city, he noticed that a traveling carnival had been set up in the park. He came to a screeching halt.

"What an eyesore!" he ranted. "I must stop people from having fun!"

He rushed into the carnival, and within a few seconds the Big Wheel, the Octopus, and the Bumper Cars were nothing but smoldering remains.

Once he reached the center of the city, Professor Gribb wreaked havoc. Within the space of a few hours he had flattened the post office, destroyed the mayor's residence, and demolished the government buildings.

By evening, the city had been declared a disaster

zone. The police had received reports of a man who was singlehandedly destroying cars and buildings, but they caught no sight of him. Professor Gribb's speed of movement made him almost invisible as he sped from place to place.

At midnight, he returned home. The satanium was beginning to wear off, and he felt awful. He was terribly tired and had a splitting headache.

On an impulse, he barged into his daughter's room. There she was, the poor bald thing, sleeping innocently.

Professor Gribb stretched out his hands and caressed her bald head.

"I'm so sorry," he said. "May all your hair grow back!"

A blue flash of electricity passed from his hands to his daughter's head. It had an immediate effect. Little worm-like creatures began to grow in all directions from her scalp. They grew longer and longer until sweet Kaylie had a flourishing headful of wormlike fingers!

"Oh, dear!" Professor Gribb said. "What have I done now? I'm so sorry!"

He realized what he must do. He rushed to his laboratory. He had to destroy the apparatus he had used to make the satanium. He raised his arms and, with a crackling flash of blue electricity, half of his laboratory was instantly reduced to ashes. It was his last act of power. He slumped to the floor and fell into a deep slumber.

In the morning, he was roused by John Feather.

"Are you all right?" he asked timidly, afraid that the professor was still keen on destroying blue-eyed people.

Professor Gribb opened one eye.

"Is that you, F . . . F . . . ?" he asked. It seemed like he couldn't remember John Feather's name.

The professor was a sorry sight. His hair was as white as a swan's feathers. His head had reduced in size somewhat but was still twice as large as it had been originally. His eyes were still tinged with gold but they were also crisscrossed with red veins. His skin was ashy gray. He was unable to think clearly about anything. His mind could no longer concentrate on any one topic for longer than eight seconds. In short, the intense energy of the satanium had fried Professor Gribb's body and mind.

Feather insisted that the professor eat something. Then he helped the professor to wash and shave himself.

Next, Feather began to tidy up the laboratory.

"What a mess!" he exclaimed.

"Yes, it is, F . . . F . . ." Professor Gribb said. "I'm sorry about that."

John Feather swept up the ashes, but among them he found the test tube containing the satanium.

"Look at this, Professor! The satanium wasn't destroyed. Perhaps it's indestructible!"

Professor Gribb looked sadly at the test tube.

But he looked sadder still when little Kaylie came running into the laboratory.

"Daddy! Daddy!" she screamed. "Look what happened to me last night!"

John Feather backed off in horror, when he saw the girl's headful of wriggling fingers.

"I still love you, K...K...K..." Barnaby said soothingly, though he could no longer remember his daughter's name.

"We must get rid of this stuff immediately," John Feather said.

"Yes," the professor agreed. "It must be sealed in concrete and thrown deep in . . ."

But the professor didn't finish his sentence. His attention had already turned elsewhere.

That same afternoon, John Feather mixed up some concrete and encased the test tube in it. The following day, when the concrete lump had dried, he drove up to Delvish Cave. The entrance had once been boarded up to prevent access, but now many of the wooden slats were missing. John Feather squeezed through into the darkness. With a flashlight, he wound his way cautiously into the dank stomach of the earth. Sleeping bats clung to the roof of the cavern in vast numbers, but they remained motionless even when John Feather lost his footing and stumbled. He just managed to avoid falling over the edge of what seemed like a pit. He shone the flashlight down, but the light merely faded in its bottomless depths. He found a small pebble and threw it in. After what seemed like ages, he heard a small splash.

"This will do just fine," John Feather said.

"Good riddance!" he shouted, as he hurled the concrete lump containing the satanium into the pit.

"Good riddance!" he heard, echoing throughout the cave.

He listened carefully. Yes, there it was. A tiny splash. The satanium was now where it could do no harm.

How wrong John Feather was!

Many years passed by. Kaylie grew up into a lovely young lady, though she always wore a hat or beret to conceal her headful of fingers. The loyal John Feather cared for Barnaby Gribb as best he could, never divulging to the world the extraordinary events he had witnessed. As for the professor . . . well, sadly he was never able to utter a complete sentence again. Periodically, though, he would mumble the words "I'm sorry . . ." and a single tear would roll from each of his eyes. These tears were collected by John Feather using an eyedropper and stored in a glass bottle on a shelf in the room that had once been the professor's laboratory. John Feather hoped one day to show the world that at least Professor Gribb was sorry for his actions.

This might have been the end of the story had it not been for the sighting of some extraordinary creatures. At first, these were considered to be just a rumor. Someone reported having seen a fox with two tails. Another person claimed to have spotted a rabbit with three ears. Yet another discovered a crow that was unable to fly because it had been born wingless.

On investigation, it became apparent that these bizarre sightings were all occurring within a ten-mile radius of Delvish Cave. Photographs began to appear in the local newspapers: a pony with claws instead of hooves; a sheep with two heads; a pig with a beak instead of a snout. Then it was discovered that all the male fish in the river below the cave had suddenly turned into females, and that all the tadpoles had grown into snails rather than frogs.

Some time later, Kaylie read about three children in a nearby suburb who had grown fingers from their heads instead of hair. Kaylie was shocked. This couldn't be a coincidence! So Kaylie began to research the problem. She felt there must be some connection between herself and the high incidence of physical abnormalities in the surrounding area.

She enrolled at the university to study astrobiophysiology. Like her father, she proved to be very, very, very, very intelligent. After she graduated, she persuaded John Feather to become her assistant.

"Mr. Feather," she said. "I believe you know more

about my father's work than you let on. I would like you to assist me in finding the cause of these physical aberrations. If we can establish the cause, we may be able to work on a cure."

"I can't," John Feather answered. "I spend all my time caring for your father. Besides that, I gave him my oath that I would never reveal the nature of his experiments."

A year later, Professor Gribb's condition deteriorated and one night he passed away quietly. At his funeral, scientists praised him for his early work and expressed their regret at his unfortunate demise. But none of them had any suspicion about his experiments with satanium, and John Feather remained silent.

The day after the funeral, Kaylie once again begged John Feather to become her assistant.

"Please help me," she begged. "For my sake and for the sake of all those other poor children who are being afflicted."

"All right," John Feather replied. "Now that I don't have any more obligations to your father."

Together, they began to restore the laboratory to its former glory. And John Feather revealed to Kaylie everything he knew about the production of satanium, about the professor's experiments during those fateful days, and of how he had disposed of the satanium in Delvish Cave.

"I am sure that the concrete casing around the

satanium has cracked or disintegrated in some way," he explained to Kaylie. "The satanium is leaking out! It must be seeping into the water table below Delvish Cave and contaminating the streams."

"We must find an antidote," Kaylie said. "If only I knew the formula my father used to produce satanium."

"I think I can help you with that," John Feather said, producing a pile of scorched notepaper from a locked cupboard. "These are what remains of Professor Gribb's notes."

Kaylie worked as hard as her father ever had, perhaps harder. She began her day at dawn, stopping only for breaks at eleven o'clock in the morning, four o'clock in the afternoon, and nine o'clock at night, during which time she would sit in her father's old wicker chair and eat a snack. All this time, she searched for the formula that would save the city from the dreadful plague that her father had introduced all those years ago.

Day after day, year after year, Kaylie produced and tested various compounds that might destroy the power of satanium. Her laboratory became filled with an extraordinary collection of orchids, mushrooms, and rare berries from the forests of Borneo. The closer she came to her goal, the more excited Kaylie became.

One morning, during her break, she exploded with joy.

"My dear Feather!" she exclaimed. "I believe I have

done it! A substance that will render satanium as harmless as a mother's milk!"

During her afternoon break, Kaylie worked out most of the formula. During the evening break, she had almost solved the problem of how to manufacture the product.

But there was still something lacking in her formula. As she sat in her father's old wicker chair late that night, she felt uneasy.

"It needs an extra something," she said to herself as she dozed off for a few moments. "Something potent . . ."

"Perhaps I can help you," she heard a voice say.

Kaylie sat up in a state of utter surprise. There, on the end of her desk, wrapped in a mantle of flames, perched a small creature. Its eyes were completely white, its ears resembled bat's wings. Its skin was scaly and its hands and feet were clawed like a bird's.

"Who are you?" Kaylie asked.

"Why, surely you recognize me," the little creature said. "I've been your inspiration all these years. The one who has given you all your best ideas."

"Nonsense!" Kaylie said. "I've never had anything to do with you!"

"Don't you dare speak to me like that!" the demon screamed. "I know what your missing ingredient is, so you had better listen to what I say."

"Get out of here!" Kaylie yelled.

The demon puffed up its chest in rage.

"I'll teach you a lesson you'll never forget!" it bellowed as it stepped toward Kaylie.

In self-defense, she reached for a bottle on the shelf nearest her. It happened to be the "I'm sorry" bottle, filled to the brim with her father's tears.

As the demon lunged toward her, Kaylie threw the liquid all over the creature.

And how the demon screamed in agony! Those tears blistered its skin, then burned deep into its body, stripping its bones of all flesh, then dissolving the bones to a puff of smoke. His mouth let out a final scream before it disappeared altogether.

There was nothing left of the demon! No trace at all.

"Wow!" Kaylie exclaimed. "These tears are powerful! I wonder if they could be the missing ingredient."

But when she examined the bottle, it was almost empty! Just a small pool of tears swished around in the bottom of the bottle. Nevertheless, she felt encouraged. She threw the tears into a pot of boiling black syrup. It bubbled into a golden froth.

Kaylie worked all night. It was still boiling in the morning when John Feather turned up for work.

"Mr. Feather, I believe we have cause for celebration this morning."

Together, they blended the antidote in the revolving tub that looked like a washing machine. The liquid was passed through spiral tubes into thick-walled chambers where laser beams flashed turquoise and yellow.

That afternoon, the first drops of the antidote were finally distilled into a small test tube. It was a victorious moment.

"Kaylie, you are a genius!" John Feather said.

"I only hope it works," Kaylie replied.

When enough antidote had been produced to fill the test tube, Kaylie held it up to the light. The liquid was almost transparent, but tinged with gold.

"Beautiful!" she remarked.

She removed the beret from her head and gazed at herself in a small hand mirror. She placed a single drop of the liquid on her scalp.

Almost immediately, the fingers on her head began to shrink. Smaller and smaller, thinner and thinner, until they shriveled away entirely.

"Wonderful, wonderful, wonderful!" John Feather exclaimed, clapping his hands and jumping up and down excitedly.

That same afternoon, Kaylie gave John Feather the test tube containing what was left of the antidote. He drove up to Delvish Cave and squeezed through the boarded-up entrance into the darkness. Using his flashlight, he found his way to the pit where he had once hurled the concrete-wrapped satanium.

He held the test tube of antidote in his hands for a moment.

"May this correct all the damage done in the past!" he said.

Then he cast the test tube into the pit.

He listened carefully. Yes, there it was. A tiny splash.

There isn't much more to tell. Half of the female fish turned back into males. Tadpoles began to grow into frogs once again. Ponies were born with hooves instead of claws; sheep were born with one head, not two; pigs were born with snouts instead of beaks. Never again were two-tailed foxes sighted, nor three-eared rabbits, nor wingless crows. In time, all the fingers growing from children's heads shrank and then disappeared.

And as for Kaylie, her head was once again covered with gorgeous golden hair.

BEHIND THE MIRROR

In the garden suburbs of Glitz City, the rich lead lives of luxury and leisure. Elegant cars cruise along opulent, tree-lined avenues before turning into long driveways that lead to huge mansions. The gardens are all perfectly cared for and some have large ponds stocked with golden fish. In one such mansion there lived a girl who had everything a person could wish for. Her name was Tyra. She lived with her mother and father and four older brothers.

Her parents were often away. Her father worked in the theater and was always on tour somewhere or other. Her mother was a businesswoman with clients in every corner of the world. They tried to make up for being away so much by bringing Tyra and her brothers expensive gifts from the countries they'd been visiting. Her brothers didn't seem to mind the arrangement — they had one another for company. But Tyra was alone much of the time, and she missed her parents terribly.

The housekeeper tried her best to look after Tyra

when the girl's parents were away. She made delicious meals for her three times a day. She put fresh flowers in Tyra's bedroom to cheer her up. And she often tried to talk to Tyra. But the girl barely responded to the housekeeper's efforts.

The huge house had once belonged to Tyra's aunt, who had been a top fashion model known as Gloria Gale. When she died, she had left the house to Tyra's mother.

There were photo albums in a cupboard containing countless photographs of Gloria Gale. Sometimes Tyra's mother showed them to Tyra. The photographs were of a slender young woman with a pretty face who was wearing extraordinary clothes. Tyra thought her aunt was beautiful, though her mother usually commented on how skinny Gloria looked. Her aunt had been very famous and glamorous when she was alive. Pictures of her were used to advertise well-known perfumes and other products.

Whenever Tyra's mother looked at the album, she wept.

"What a tragic waste!" she would say through her tears. "She was so young."

Tyra often wandered through the corridors and rooms of this house. In fact, there were thirty-two rooms altogether, including the gym with its exercise machines, the indoor swimming pool, and the photography studio. Some rooms were seldom used, some never. There was one room, in particular, that Tyra was always afraid to enter. This was her aunt's bedroom, left the way it had been when she was still alive. There was a large bed in the center of the room and built-in closets all around, with her aunt's fashionable garments still hanging inside them. Tyra felt uncomfortable there, so she avoided the room at all times.

One morning, Tyra awoke feeling ill. Her parents were both away in foreign countries. Her brothers had gone off to college. She looked in her mirror and saw the reflection of a girl who wasn't as pretty and slender as her famous aunt. Tyra decided she was too sick to go to school that day, so she stayed in bed until lunchtime. By mid-afternoon she was bored. She was fed up with all her belongings, even the new electronic keyboard that her parents had given her when they'd last been home.

Suddenly, she heard a distant voice calling.

"Tyra! Tyra! Don't be so glum and gloomy. Come up here, dear!"

It was a woman's voice. But who could it be? There was nobody else at home apart from Tyra and the housekeeper, and it certainly wasn't the housekeeper.

Tyra was petrified, but there was something compelling in that voice, something hypnotic that forced her to jump out of bed, put on her robe, and walk out of her room into the hallway.

She heard the voice again.

"Come up the stairs, sweetie! Do as I say!"

As if in a trance, Tyra obeyed.

"In here!" the voice said. It seemed to be coming from Gloria Gale's bedroom!

Tyra couldn't believe it. Her body trembled with fear.

"Don't be afraid, honey! Turn the handle!"

Tyra didn't want to enter that room, but there was an incredible sorcery in that voice that forced her to turn the handle on the bedroom door and step inside.

"Tyra! How you've grown!"

Tyra couldn't see anyone in the room. But the voice was louder now.

"We're having a party in here and you're invited!"

"Who's speaking to me?" Tyra whispered. "Where are you?"

"I'm here, sweetheart!" the voice said. "Come nearer!"

The voice seemed to be coming from the full-length mirror on the far side of the room. Tyra wanted to leave. She didn't want to go nearer. But there was a power in the voice that forced her to step across the room.

She looked in the mirror but couldn't see anything other than her own image.

Again she heard the voice. It seemed to be coming from the mirror or from behind it.

"You can't come to the party in a robe!" the voice said. "Go put on one of those lovely dresses. Something white, I think."

Tyra didn't want to try on any of Gloria Gale's dresses, but the eerie voice compelled her to open one of the wardrobes. Within a short time, she changed into a stylish white silk dress, wrapped a fringed white scarf around her neck, and slipped into a pair of white shoes.

Tyra examined herself in the full-length mirror. Her aunt's dress didn't fit perfectly, but she thought she looked quite glamorous. The voice said, "How lovely!"

"Where are you?" Tyra asked. "I can't see you!"

"Look carefully, dear!" the voice said.

It was then that Tyra noticed a small gap in the center of the mirror, where a tiny fragment had chipped away. The crack was only as broad as a pencil, but Tyra put her eye up against it and peeped through.

What a shock Tyra received! There, on the other side of the mirror, in a huge room, was the owner of the mysterious voice!

Tyra recognized her immediately. It was none other than Gloria Gale! Her aunt was standing there looking straight back at Tyra. Her aunt's eyes had dark rings around them, as if they'd been painted with charcoal, and her cheeks were so pale they seemed to be dusted with chalk.

Behind Gloria were hundreds of guests, all slim and dressed in the latest fashions. They were all having a good time, it seemed. Some were dancing, others were chatting and laughing. Still others were preening themselves in front of oval mirrors.

Tyra was so frightened, she was nearly paralyzed.

"Come join us!" Gloria urged Tyra, beckoning with her finger.

"How?" Tyra asked.

"Just climb through the crack, honey!"

Tyra didn't want to, but her aunt's voice was too powerful for her. Tyra had to try. But how was it possible? The crack was so narrow. Not even her little finger would fit through that tiny gap.

"Oh, you silly child!" Gloria said. "You're much too plump! You'll never fit through!"

Tyra didn't like being insulted. Tears formed in her eyes. Gloria Gale's voice boomed out at her.

"In the future, you're to eat nothing that's white!"

"What do you mean?" Tyra asked.

"You must not eat food that has any white ingredients in it! Now go away at once!"

The voice of her aunt rang out its evil spell. Tyra felt a dreadful pain rush through her body as she realized she had no choice but to do as she'd been told.

The housekeeper wasn't pleased.

"Oh, heaven help us! What's come over you? Nothing white? No bread? No cakes?"

But Tyra insisted and that was that. From now on, the

housekeeper had to make meals and snacks without rice or flour or sugar or milk or salt.

It was difficult for Tyra to miss out on so many of her favorite foods, but she couldn't help herself.

After a month, Tyra had lost a quarter of her weight.

Then one afternoon, to her horror, she heard that terrible voice again. She knew it was Gloria Gale calling to her. She had to obey.

Up she went again to her aunt's bedroom.

"Put on one of those lovely dresses!" the voice suggested. "Something red."

The voice was irresistible. Tyra changed into a red silk dress, wrapped a red fringed scarf around her neck, and slipped into a pair of red shoes.

Tyra examined herself in the full-length mirror. Her aunt's dress still didn't fit properly. Her face looked sallow now that her cheeks had lost some of their color and shape.

"How lovely!" the voice said. "Come and join us!"

Tyra felt she had no choice but to obey. But how could she? Not even her little finger would fit through that tiny gap.

"You're still too plump, you silly child!" Gloria Gale said. "In the future, not only will you avoid white foods, but you will also eat nothing red. Is that clear?"

Tyra felt sick when she heard this! But the spell was

so powerful. Tyra knew that she would have to do as she'd been told.

The housekeeper was extremely upset.

"Heavens above! Whatever next? Nothing red? No ketchup? No bacon?"

But Tyra seemed to have made up her mind, so the housekeeper prepared meals without meat, tomatoes, cherries, plums, or strawberries.

Again it was painful for Tyra to miss out on so many delicious foods, but she couldn't help herself.

After a month, Tyra had lost half her weight.

Then one afternoon, to her dismay, she heard Gloria Gale calling to her again. The evil voice had to be obeyed.

Up she went to her aunt's bedroom. This time the voice demanded that she dress in yellow. Tyra changed into a yellow silk dress, wrapped a yellow fringed scarf around her neck, and slipped into a pair of yellow shoes.

She examined herself in the mirror. Her aunt's dress still didn't fit perfectly, and she was startled by her own pale and sickly image.

But the voice said, "How lovely! You're looking better and better! Do come and join us!"

As if in a bad dream, Tyra had to obey. Yet, how could she? Not even her little finger would fit through that tiny gap.

"You're still too plump, you silly child!" Gloria Gale said. "In the future, not only will you avoid red and white foods, but you will also eat nothing yellow!"

Tyra felt so weak she almost fainted, but her aunt's magical voice wouldn't release its grip on her. Tyra was forced to do as she'd been told.

The housekeeper was very distressed.

"Lord have mercy, child! You're wasting away! Nothing yellow? No custard? No omelettes?"

But Tyra did what the voice told her to do. The housekeeper had to find recipes without cheese, butter, eggs, lemons, or corn.

Tyra hated the food she was presented with. It barely had any taste. But she couldn't help herself.

After a month, Tyra had lost three-quarters of her weight.

Then one afternoon — oh, no! — she heard Gloria Gale calling to her again. As if she were sleepwalking, Tyra obeyed.

Up she went again to her aunt's bedroom. This time, the voice commanded her to dress in green. Tyra changed into a green silk dress, wrapped a green fringed scarf around her neck, and slipped into a pair of green shoes.

She examined herself in the mirror. She barely recognized her image, with its hollow eyes and sunken cheeks, wearing a dress that almost fit but not quite.

"How lovely!" the evil voice said. "You're looking elegant! Now come and join us!"

Tyra didn't want to, but the magic in that terrible voice forced her to try and climb through the crack in the mirror.

Yet how could she? Not even her little finger would fit through that tiny gap.

"You're still too plump, you silly child!" Gloria Gale said. "In the future, not only will you avoid yellow, red, and white foods, but you will also eat nothing green!"

Tyra was shocked. How would she survive? But the evil voice of her aunt had to be obeyed.

The housekeeper was beside herself with worry.

"What the devil's wrong with you, child? What will your parents say? They'll think it's all my fault. Nothing green? No vegetables? No salads?"

But Tyra insisted. The housekeeper despaired.

"You poor waif! If you don't eat lettuce or peas or broccoli or celery or cucumbers, what on Earth will you eat?"

It soon became clear. Tyra didn't eat anything at all! She drank only water, which was transparent and had no color.

It was torment to eat nothing. She longed for the delicious foods that the housekeeper used to cook.

After a month she weighed almost nothing at all.

Then one awful afternoon, Tyra heard the terrible

voice that she had hoped she would never hear again. There was no resisting it. She had to obey.

Up she went to her aunt's bedroom. This time, the voice instructed her to dress in black. Tyra changed into a black silk dress, wrapped a black fringed scarf around her neck, and slipped into a pair of black shoes.

She examined herself in the mirror. This time, her aunt's dress fit perfectly! But the girl she saw in the mirror looked so wasted and sad!

Despite this, the voice said, "How lovely! You look fabulous! Come and join us!"

Tyra burst out weeping, but her aunt's voice was powerful.

"Climb through the crack!" it shrieked.

Tyra approached the mirror. And this time her little finger fit through the tiny gap! She was terrified! Surely the rest of her wouldn't fit through.

Just as she was wondering about this, she felt her little finger being gripped from the other side of the mirror. Gloria Gale was tugging on her finger, heaving and pulling her through the crack. Tyra struggled desperately to stay on her side of the mirror.

"Come through, sweetheart!" Gloria intoned as she tugged on Tyra's finger.

Oh, that voice! That terrible, terrible voice! Its powerful, evil magic sapped Tyra of her strength. She was losing the struggle!

Suddenly, with a lot of squeezing and pain — *plop* — she fell through to the other side.

"I'm so glad you've come to join us," Gloria Gale said. "My, you do look gorgeous!"

Tyra was now able to see her aunt close-up — the famous Gloria Gale, slim and pretty, just as she appeared in all the photographs. But there was something so frightening about her! She looked like nothing but skin and bones to Tyra — her cheeks were pale and sunken, her eyes hollow and glazed.

In fact, Gloria Gale was so thin and weightless, she cast no shadow on the floor, despite the light blazing down on her from the crystal chandelier above. A cold chill passed through Tyra's body. She turned to examine the other guests and soon realized that not one person in the room was casting a shadow!

Oh, no! What about herself? She looked down at the ground in front of her feet. No sign of a shadow! She looked to the left, to the right, and behind her. No shadow at all!

"There are so many people I'd like you to meet," Gloria Gale said, introducing Tyra first to one person, then another.

Many young men came to say hello to Tyra and she was polite to them all. But how cold their hands were! Cold as corpses. And how pale their faces! Except for the dark rings around their eyes.

The chattering and laughing continued endlessly. Conversations about nothing in particular, jokes that weren't really funny, although people laughed as if they were. Every so often one of the guests would comb her hair in front of one of the many mirrors in the room, or would disappear for a few moments, only to return in a new outfit, keeping up with the latest fashions.

The longer Tyra was there, the more she lost track of time, until she barely knew if hours were passing, or days, or months, or even years. One moment was exactly like the next and nothing ever changed, except for the clothes.

It occurred to Tyra that she was trapped in a world where nothing and nobody was real. If only she could escape from this endless party! But every door led only to a dressing room. There was no way out!

In the meantime, Tyra's mother and father returned from abroad. The housekeeper had contacted them urgently, sobbing with anguish as she told them that Tyra had vanished. She had searched the house but had found only discarded clothes.

Tyra's parents were overcome with grief and remorse. They contacted the police, but they also could find no trace of Tyra.

"It's all our fault!" Tyra's mother wept. "We didn't take good care of her."

"We should never have left her on her own so much," her father wailed. "We may never see our daughter again."

"Oh, no, don't say that," her mother said, sobbing.

Tyra's four brothers were also upset.

"We should have kept an eye on her," they admitted. "Now we must go out into the world and search for her."

The brothers left the rich suburb of Glitz City and journeyed for one year and a day in search of their sister. North, south, east, and west they each went, but there was no sign of Tyra anywhere! However, on their travels, each of the brothers married and they brought their four young brides back to live in the enormous house.

The wives got along well together. They spent a lot of time in one another's company, singing songs and learning about life in the four corners of the world. Although it was a sad house to live in, the four wives kept themselves happy and in good spirits.

One day they were exploring the large house when they heard a voice calling from upstairs.

"Come up here, my dears!"

The four wives were astonished. But there was something compelling in the voice that forced them to go upstairs.

The voice was coming from Gloria Gale's bedroom!

"In here, my honeys!" the voice said.

The four wives shook with fear.

"Don't be afraid, sweeties, we're having a party and you're all invited!"

The four ladies didn't want to enter that room, but

some terrible power in the voice forced them to turn the handle on the bedroom door and step inside.

"Come join the party!" the voice called from behind the full-length mirror.

The four wives hesitated, but the evil voice forced them to walk across the room.

"Oh, you can't come to the party in those old dresses!" the voice said. "Go and find yourself some lovely dresses in that closet."

The four ladies knew there was something very odd going on, but the hypnotic voice persuaded them to open the closet and dress in four glamorous outfits that didn't fit properly.

"How lovely you all look," the voice said. "Now, come on through!"

"Through where?" they all asked.

"Through the crack in the mirror!" the voice commanded.

The four ladies each put an eye to the crack, one after another, and peeped through. There, on the other side, was the owner of the evil voice — Gloria Gale, with her hollow eyes and sunken cheeks — beckoning with her finger for them to come through the mirror.

"Through this small gap!" They laughed. "You must be joking! We can't fit through there."

"That's because you're all too plump, you silly girls!" the voice said.

The lady from the north, dressed in white, examined herself in the full-length mirror.

"You think I'm too plump, do you?" she said to Gloria Gale.

"Without a doubt! And in the future," Gloria Gale commanded, "you're to eat nothing that's white! Do you understand?"

"What twaddle!" said the lady from the north. "I like myself just the way I am."

She threw off the white dress and put on her own clothes.

The lady from the south, dressed in red, examined herself in the mirror.

"You surely don't think I'm too plump?"

"You most certainly are!" the evil voice replied. "From now on you're to eat nothing that's red!"

"Nonsense!" said the lady from the south. "I enjoy my food and I feel good."

She immediately discarded the red dress and put on her own clothes.

The lady from the east, dressed in yellow, examined herself in the mirror.

"It's not me that's plump! It's this dress that's so small it would only fit a stick!"

"Of course it's not the dress, you fathead!" fumed the evil voice. "In the future you're to eat nothing that's yellow!"

"Don't be absurd!" exclaimed the lady from the east. "You can't tell me what to do!"

She flung off the yellow dress and put on her own clothes.

The lady from the west, dressed in green, examined herself in the mirror.

"Plump, shmump! Who cares anyway?"

"I do!" the evil voice cried. "From now on you're to eat nothing that's green!"

"How ridiculous!" said the lady from the west. "I certainly don't want to end up looking dead like you do!"

With that, she took off the green dress and put on her own clothes.

Then the four ladies burst out laughing — Gloria Gale's spell had lost all its power.

"We've never heard anything so ridiculous in all our lives."

They turned their backs on the mirror and were about to leave the room when they heard a tiny voice squeaking, "Help! Help!"

They looked around to find a finger poking through the crack in the mirror.

"Please help me! She's a witch! Pull me through!"

The lady from the north grabbed hold of the finger and began to pull. Then the lady from the south took hold of her. The lady from the east also began to pull, and finally the lady from the west grabbed hold, too.

But on the other side of the mirror, Gloria Gale had grabbed onto Tyra and was holding her fiercely.

"Pull harder!" Tyra called.

All four women pulled and pulled, until with a great heave a young girl came squeezing through the crack and — *plop!* — she landed in the room with them.

"Thank you, thank you!" she said. "It was so awful in there!"

The voice of Gloria Gale came shrieking through the hole in the mirror. "Don't think I'm finished with you!"

"Who are you?" the four women asked the young girl.

"I'm Tyra," the girl explained.

"Tyra! Our sister-in-law!" The four ladies rejoiced. "You've come back to us!"

They hugged Tyra and danced around the room with her. Tyra didn't even notice that her shadow had returned and was dancing around the room beneath her feet.

"You poor thing," said the lady from the north. "You're so frail."

"You're nothing but skin and bones," said the lady from the south.

"You look like you haven't had a good meal in months," said the lady from the east.

"We'll help you to get well again," said the lady from the west.

When Tyra had changed out of the black dress into her own clothes, they took her downstairs.

What a rejoicing there was when Tyra's mother and father and brothers saw her again!

The housekeeper was beside herself with happiness. "Oh, thank goodness! What a relief! Please can I cook you food with colors again?" she asked.

"Yes, let's have something to eat right now to celebrate!" Tyra's mother suggested.

The housekeeper laid the table and the family sat down.

A plate of food was placed in front of Tyra. But just as she was about to lift some to her mouth, she heard a voice calling down to her from her aunt's bedroom.

"You're too plump to eat, you silly girl!"

Tyra hesitated. She put the food back on the plate.

"I don't want to be like my aunt," Tyra exclaimed. "But what can I do?"

"Just start with a little of each color," her mother suggested.

Tyra lifted the food to her mouth. The four wives smiled and cheered as Tyra nibbled snacks that were white, red, yellow, and green.

"My darling daughter!" her mother said, wrapping her arms around her.

On a day much like any other day, a father much like any other father and a daughter much like any other daughter went out for a walk. The daughter's name was Nayette.

They lived on the edge of the city, so the countryside was within reach by walking. They walked through the park, around the supermarket, over the railway bridge, across the farm, and there they were, beyond the sprawling suburbs of the city.

They were walking up the gentle rise, through the pastures where sheep were grazing, when a tall, red-bearded fellow with a backpack and a walking stick came striding toward them.

"Good day to you," he greeted them amiably.

"And to you, too," Nayette's father answered.

"Oh, are you in for a surprise today!" the fellow said. "If you take the path from Abbick that leads across the hills to Zander you will be amazed."

"We weren't going to go that far," Nayette's father said.

"Oh, you should, you should," the tall fellow said enthusiastically. "The place is magical."

"Let's go there, Daddy," Nayette pleaded.

"Okay, sweetheart," the father replied.

The red-bearded fellow smiled and passed them on his way into the city. He went the way they had come, across the farm, over the railway bridge, around the supermarket, and through the park.

They went the way he had come, up the steep path in the direction of Zander.

When they reached the crest of the first ridge, they gazed back at the city. Somewhere among that sea of roofs was their own house.

That thought disturbed Nayette's father.

"Oh, no!" he exclaimed to himself. "I left the front door of the house unlocked!"

For a moment he considered turning back. But then he figured that by then they were so far from home that it was almost as well to go ahead to Zander. From there they could get a taxi to take them home.

So as not to trouble his daughter, he kept these thoughts to himself. But how uncomfortable he felt! He could easily see in his mind's eye that with the door of the house unlocked, a burglar could get in. With no one else in the house, a burglar would have plenty of time to rummage through all the drawers and cupboards of the house and steal whatever he wanted.

While her father was absorbed in these imaginings, a glint of golden light caught Nayette's eye. She turned to see what it was. There, a little way off in a field, was a bird of unusual beauty, the feathers of its wings glinting gold in the sunlight. Nayette knew immediately what it was — a jula-bird. Her late mother had once told her about jula-birds, how extraordinary they were, and how rare.

Nayette stared and stared as the bird pecked around in the long grass. It was only then that Nayette glimpsed a similar bird just a short distance away from the first. As she focused her gaze on the second bird, she noticed a third, a fourth, and a fifth. In fact, the long grass was teeming with jula-birds. How had she failed to notice them until now? There were so many of them, gleaming golden as they strutted here and there.

Then, almost as if one of them had given a command, they all fluttered softly into the air. What a magnificent sight! The whole flock moved in harmony, as if they were a single creature, flying one way and then the other, rising all the while into the blue sky. As they swung to the left, their wings shone golden, and as they swung to the right, silver!

Nayette had to shield her eyes from their brightness.

It was as if she were gazing into an ocean reflecting the sun's rays. Nayette was certain she had never before seen any birds quite so beautiful.

They all flew off into the distance, dancing in formation across the sky, and then with one last golden glint, they disappeared behind the next hill and were gone from sight.

Nayette walked on quietly beside her father. He was anxiously scratching the top of his head as if he could encourage his brain to remember whether he had locked the front door or not.

How stupid of me! he thought.

That burglar could be in the house by now, going through all the rooms. The father pictured the burglar stealing all their clothes and the camera he kept on the top shelf of his closet. It was quite a new camera and had cost a lot, even though he'd bought it on sale. The burglar would probably take all his most treasured possessions and load them into a van — his CD player, his piano, his TV, his computers. Everything!

Nayette and her father walked on over the high ridge and arrived at a small sheltered valley that lay bathed in sunlight.

"It's lovely here, isn't it?" Nayette said to her father.

"Yes, darling," her father responded, taking hold of her hand. He scanned the scenery for a moment, but soon became absorbed in his thoughts again.

In the center of the valley, just ahead of them, was an imposing tree.

Nayette released her hand from her father's and ran toward the tree. She walked all the way around it, gasping with astonishment. The branches were resplendent with buds, each the size of a plum and in appearance just like a flame — red and orange and yellow. Nayette stared and stared. To her astonishment, right in front of her very eyes, one of the buds began to unfold. Slowly, perfectly, it unwrapped its glossy petals, stretching them gracefully, like a fist opening its fingers. From the center of the bloom an exquisite scent wafted to Nayette's nostrils, a scent sweeter and more delicate than any perfume in any store in the whole wide world. Almost immediately, a small hummingbird started probing the flower with its long beak, curved exactly so that it could suck out the delicious nectar within.

When the bird was done, the flower began to pale. The colors faded from its petals and within seconds shriveled and fell to the ground.

Nayette was shocked to discover how short-lived the beauty of the flower was. She had hoped it might last forever. But then, as suddenly as the first flower had bloomed, a second one began to unfold its petals. Nayette was enchanted! Another hummingbird arrived and sucked the nectar within the flower, and again the petals faded and dropped to the ground.

Almost immediately, a third began to flower. Slowly its petals opened. Nayette thought the tree was like fireworks in slow motion, shooting out colorful rockets, which then faded and fell to the ground.

Nayette was filled with wonder and was certain she had never before set eyes upon a tree quite so beautiful.

"Come on, Nayette!" she heard her father call. "We can't waste time here."

Nayette was reluctant to leave the fireworks tree, but she knew she had to. She joined her father again on the path. He was fishing around in his jacket pockets, searching for something. His car keys! He couldn't find them. *How stupid!* he thought.

If the burglar got into the house, then he'd probably find the keys in his desk and steal the car, his pride and joy. Not only that, if the burglar rummaged through his desk, he'd find his checkbook and be able to withdraw all their money. Nayette's father was consumed with misery but said nothing about all this to his daughter, not wishing to upset her.

They walked on together, Nayette and her father, until they entered the gorge. Tall rock cliffs rose on either side of them. Nayette thought she heard something. She stopped for a moment to listen. Her father paced on ahead. She could hear a sort of whispering, singing sound.

She stepped forward again and followed the twists

and turns that the path took through the gorge. The whispered singing was getting nearer.

As she turned the next bend, a tremendous noise like a great symphony orchestra assailed her ears. Before her was an enormous waterfall! So high was the cliff over which it plunged that it seemed to be dropping from the sky itself. Nayette looked up and saw small rainbows playing in the mists from the falling waters.

She was riveted to the spot. She stared and stared. Never had she experienced anything like this before! Or heard anything quite so magnificent! Wherever the tumbling water struck a rock, it uttered a singing sound. And all the water together combined to produce the most majestic music, swirling with different themes, sometimes booming and deep, at other times, tinkling like miniature bells.

"Nayette, are you coming or are you going to stand there forever?"

It was her father, shouting to make his voice be heard over the music of the falls.

"It's getting late," he said.

Nayette wished she could spend forever listening to the waterfall music. She was certain she had never before heard any music quite so beautiful.

Nayette's father suggested that she walk quickly up the damp, stone steps. He wanted to get home as soon as possible. It would probably be too late, anyway. The burglar would have already stolen everything. Nayette's father could see it all in his mind: The family would descend into poverty. Without money or a car he would probably lose his job. He would have to sell the house in order to survive with Nayette. He would be forced to live in a rental apartment. Would he even be able to provide Nayette with enough food to eat?

The steps carved in the rock were slippery and steep. They led up from the waterfall to the summit of Zander Point. Up and up they wound, eventually broadening out onto a high plateau overlooking the countryside below. Tall columns of rock stood around them like giant guards.

Nayette breathed the air deeply and took in the splendid view. As she did so, she suddenly spotted a white animal grazing on the slopes behind some young fir trees. The animal shied away as her father stomped past.

But Nayette longed to see the creature again. She slowed down and, as if she were wearing velvet slippers, softly tiptoed off the path toward the fir trees. Then she stood very still holding her breath, her eyes as wide as teacups.

She watched and waited. After a while, a small white hoof stepped into view from behind a tree. This was followed by what appeared to be a small white gazelle, with beautiful, gentle eyes.

Nayette stared and stared. She could scarcely believe

what she was seeing — a young gazelle with a single horn in the middle of its forehead!

It looked up at Nayette. She thought the creature might flee when it saw a human being. But it didn't. Instead it took another step forward, and another, approaching ever closer to Nayette.

Eventually, it reached her. Nayette didn't move a muscle. The creature lowered its head. Slowly and deliberately it touched Nayette's arm with its elegant, spiral-patterned horn.

It was an amazing feeling. Nayette's arm glowed with a warmth that spread up to her shoulders and then radiated across into her whole body. Nayette's heart nearly burst with pleasure.

"I told you we need to hurry!" Nayette's father shouted irritably, coming back up the path to get her.

Instantly, the unicorn gazelle bounded off into the darkness of the forest.

Tears fell from Nayette's eyes. Her father had scared off the wonderful creature.

But still, she was grateful to have seen it. She was certain she had never before seen an animal quite so beautiful. Its touch had changed her forever. She knew something special had happened. In that single moment, it was as if the creature had chosen her to be the recipient of its love.

Nayette's father fumed on the way down the

mountainside. He was not only concerned about how long the walk had taken, but he was distraught by what he knew would happen to his daughter if all their money had been stolen by the burglar. He clearly saw that Nayette would have to walk around in ragged clothing and that social workers would come to take her away from him. He was almost weeping by the time he and Nayette descended into Zander.

On the outskirts of the little village, a man came striding toward them. It was the tall red-bearded fellow with the backpack and walking stick whom they had seen before.

"Did you have a good time?" he asked.

"Oh, yes," Nayette said. "The path was magical."

"Was it?" her father asked.

"Yes," Nayette said. "We saw the golden jula-birds and the fireworks tree. We heard the waterfall music and best of all was the unicorn gazelle. It even touched me with its horn."

"We saw nothing of the sort," Nayette's father said. "Don't make up such nonsense."

"I'm not!" Nayette insisted.

"Anyway, we have to go home," Nayette's father said, "because I have important business to get back to."

Nayette said good-bye to the bearded fellow.

"Thanks for telling us to take that path," she said gratefully.

Nayette's father took hold of Nayette's hand and led her quickly down the path.

But suddenly he stopped.

"How terrible!" he said. "I've just understood."

"What?" Nayette asked.

"Don't you see?" he said. "That man's the burglar."

"Which man?"

"That red-bearded man who told us to take the path from Abbick to Zander."

"Of course he isn't," Nayette said.

"Don't you see?" her father explained. "He told us to take that path so that he would have the time to go to our house and steal all our belongings."

"No, he didn't," Nayette said. "He's a lovely man."

"You'll see," Nayette's father said. "Let's hurry!"

They made their way down into Zander where Nayette's father hired a taxi that he ordered to zoom back to their house.

"Faster, faster!" he ordered the taxi driver.

Eventually, they arrived home. Nayette's father paid the taxi driver, then rushed to his front door.

It was locked. He hadn't left it unlocked after all. And no burglar had come, nor had anything been stolen.

"I'm sorry I thought badly of the red-bearded man," Nayette's father said, hugging his daughter. "Do you think one day we could try walking the path again?"

A child in the mirror sees a beast,
a beast in the mirror sees an outcast,
an outcast in the mirror sees a rebel.

A rebel in the mirror sees a coward,
a coward in the mirror sees a soldier,
a soldier in the mirror sees a captive.

A captive in the mirror sees a bride,
a bride in the mirror sees a gambler,
a gambler in the mirror sees a hero.

A hero in the mirror sees a child.

About the Author

Silverman is a pen name.
The real identity of the author
remains a closely guarded secret.

SONG QUEST *by Katherine Roberts*

Far from the Purple Plains and the Mountains of Midnight, nestled in the crystal-blue waters of the Western Sea, lies the Isle of Echoes, where the forces of good and evil are held in harmony by a strange and mysterious people: the Singers. The Singers can hear the silent voices of magical half-creatures and can speak over great distances using only their minds. But a great evil threatens to destroy their isle and all that is good in the world.

This is the debut title in *The Echorium Sequence.*

"It was a big beach, and the three friends soon left the rest of the class behind. As they wandered along the tide line, Chissar and Frenn darted back and forth, digging up pieces of broken shell and popping the seaweed pods, teasing each other they'd found things when all they had were handfuls of silver sand containing tiny specks of bluestone. Rialle walked slowly, eyes half-closed. Her head was throbbing now, like one of the drums their teachers used to keep rhythm, yet she couldn't stop thinking about Singer Graia's words.

Use all your senses. Use your ears."

CRYSTAL MASK *by Katherine Roberts*

Twenty years after the events described in *Song Quest*, enemies of The Echorium are once again growing strong. Renn, the novice Singer, and Shaiala, the girl raised by centaurs, must find a way to conquer an evil power that has enslaved the half-creatures and Two-Hoof children —a power that can bend minds and steal memory.

"By the time she'd scrambled down to the canyon floor, all her friends had been driven through the crevice. She ran through after them. The sight beyond brought her to a halt. Nearly a hundred exhausted, frightened centaur foals shivered in the natural trap formed by the inner canyon, hobbled and taunted by Two Hoofs."

SPELLFALL *by Katherine Roberts*

Someone knows Natalie is special. He knows her mother came from Earthhaven, the mysterious world that lies beyond the Thrallstone. He knows her father is a Thrall who sells spells between the two worlds. And now the exiled Spellmage wants her power.

"Natalie saw the first spell in the supermarket parking lot. It was floating in a puddle near the recycling bins, glimmering bronze and green in the October drizzle. At first she thought it was a leaf, though as she drew closer it began to look more like a crumpled candy wrapper — a very interesting candy wrapper. *Pick me up*, it seemed to say, glittering intriguingly. *Surely I'm worth a closer look*. She shook her head and hurried past. She was wet and cold and had more things to worry about than picking up someone else's trash. But the trap had been baited by one who knew a lot more about spells than she did."

THE WITCH TRADE *by Michael Molloy*

Meet Abby, Spike, Captain Starlight, and Benbow, his faithful albatross. Together with Sir Chadwick, the flamboyant leader of the Light Witches, they piece together an ancient map and journey across shark-infested seas, to discover the hidden source of Black Witch power!

" 'I thought witches were only in fairy tales,' said Abby doubtfully. 'Oh, no.' The captain shook his head. 'There's always been witches —good ones and bad ones. And, what's more, they've been battling each other forever.' "

THE TIME WITCHES *by Michael Molloy*

Wolfbane, the escaped leader of the evil Night Witches, and his evil mother plot revenge on the heroes Abby and Spike. Between them, they conspire to summon up a long dead witch who knows the secret of time travel, allowing them to go back in time to change the course of events that led to their downfall.
This is the exciting sequel to *The Witch Trade*.

"Abby looked in the direction of the Darkwood Forest and saw storm clouds rolling toward them. There was a strange light in the sky. High above, Benbow circled. He seemed to be calling out a warning. A dark shape was growing in the sky. The wind was so strong now they could hardly stand. The air filled with a dreadful howling — it sounded like a thousand people shrieking in agony. The menacing shape in the sky took on a recognizable shape. Abby shouted out a warning, but it was too late. Ma Hemlock's spectral carriage was upon them."